DIAMONDBACK McCALL: ISLAND LOST

Other books by Robert Middleton:

Diamondback McCall

DIAMONDBACK McCALL: ISLAND LOST

•

Robert Middleton

AVALON BOOKS
NEW YORK

Published by Thomas Bouregy & Co., Inc.
160 Madison Avenue, New York, NY 10016

Library of Congress Cataloging-in-Publication Data

Middleton, Robert, 1950–
    Diamondback McCall—island lost / Robert Middleton.
        p. cm.
    ISBN 978-0-8034-9850-1 (hardcover : acid-free paper)
    I. Title.

PS3613.I3625D53 2007
813'.6—dc22

                                          2007013581

PRINTED IN THE UNITED STATES OF AMERICA
ON ACID-FREE PAPER
BY HADDON CRAFTSMEN, BLOOMSBURG, PENNSYLVANIA

To my good friend, Larry Chaney,
who willingly gave so much of his time and talent,
my deepest appreciation.

For their thoughtful comments and suggestions,
my sincere thanks to the following special people:

Denise Middleton
Carol Biller
Rick Ciauri
John Jones
Rita and Larry Bittner
Skip Middleton

Foreword

Some men gain their reputations as lawmen. Others, as hired guns and cold-blooded killers. Jack "Diamondback" McCall became famous, with his lightning-quick draw, as the star in a traveling show.

It could be said that he came by his considerable talent honestly. Both of his parents were circus performers. His mother, a gymnast and trapeze artist. His father, a quick draw and trickshot performer.

Jack was ten when his father began teaching him how to use a gun. He practiced tirelessly, and the pupil ultimately surpassed the teacher. His father also evoked an adherence to the code of the West. It was a strict code of honor, where a man lived by his word, measured out swift justice, and treated women with courtly kindness. That was the kind of man that Jack became. A man intolerant of breaches in the code, and good enough to set it right.

He lost his mother to yellow fever when he was

twelve. His father's end came five years later. It took Jack some months to track down the three men who had backshot him. He settled the score by taking all three at once. For the next couple years, he simply wandered before eventually joining the traveling show.

During his time with the show, men would inevitably come to take him on, sometimes several at a time. The result was equally inevitable. They came looking to gain a reputation, but ended up only causing Jack's to grow.

Since leaving the show, he had found two good friends, a lost city, and the love of his life.

Dakota Dan Smith had once been a deputy. They were now partners. Dan had a round, friendly face. He wore his off-white Stetson tilted way back. Tan suspenders passed over his well-worn white shirt and portly torso. His holster carried a single .45 Colt, but his partner usually did the shooting. Jack could always count on the chubby old-timer to be humorous, amiable, and ready to back him up.

Fawn was the most beautiful and clever girl he had ever known. She was from the Papago tribe, but brought up by cattle ranchers who had lost their own little girl. She was bright and articulate. They were very much in love.

Chota belonged to a lost and secret tribe. A single feather graced his long black hair. He wore the alabaster-colored clothing that was customary for his people. Although not physically strong, he was one of the very few in his tribe trusted to leave their hidden city. When Jack first saw Chota, he stood up for him, and managed to humiliate a powerful rancher, Brad

Barlow, in the process. When Barlow sent his private Army after Jack, Chota was forced to lead Jack, along with Dan and Fawn, to his village called Spirit Feather. Jack now thought of the Anasazi city, deep within a mountain cavern, as his home.

When Jack discovered the underground lake and geyser beneath the Anasazi city, he put to rest the villagers' long held belief in a demon known as Qualtari. Since then, the lake beneath the city had become a haven for the Anasazi to fish and swim.

Jack was always welcomed by the Anasazi; there was little he wouldn't do for them.

Diamondback McCall was tall and powerfully built, looking all the more so aboard his big palomino stallion, Chilco. He was known for his black attire adorned with snakeskin hatband, belt, and boots. He was feared for his two pearl-handled Colts and his astonishing speed. The .45 caliber pistols resided in low-slung black holsters with the initials JDM in silver letters.

Men would think of the tall, dark *hombre* as imposing. Women would call him handsome.

Chapter 1
Vengeance

It was mid-morning and already getting hot. Riders passed by, their horses stirring the powder-dry street of the Mexican bordertown. Dust hung in the air. The summer of 1884 wore on.

Jack and Dakota Dan found some escape from the heat in a small, and rather pleasant, cantina. Classic Spanish style would describe it. Its thick adobe walls and high tile roof kept the temperature down. Inside were the usual smells and sounds of a saloon, but with a simple Mexican charm. Sunlight peered in from a few small arched windows, as well as the doorway, which was of the swinging variety, more commonly found in the North. Directly across from the doors was the bar, tended by a middle-aged bartender. He was small and thin. Behind him was a large mirror above assorted bottles and kegs.

Jack and Dan had two mugs before them. They stood on the far right side of the bar, Jack's preferred spot. A man like Diamondback McCall would never show his back to a doorway.

It had been Dan's idea to ride down to this sleepy bordertown. He needed a new pair of boots, and Nogales was famous for their bootmakers. Jack had just come along to keep him company. The cobbler had said Dan's boots would be finished in an hour or so. They had some time to kill.

Forty minutes and a couple brews later, Jack's attention was drawn to three men standing in the doorway. He could see them clearly enough in the mirror, but he turned to look their way. They had stopped before the swinging doors. The man in the center leaned over the doors and gave the place a look from side to side. When his eyes met Jack's, they stopped.

Jack didn't know these men, but it seemed obvious that the one in the middle knew him.

He pushed the doors aside and headed straight for Jack and Dan. He stopped a few feet in front of them. His two amigos came up from behind. They now stood there, three abreast. Jack stepped away from the bar, and turned to face them. Dan did the same.

There were only a half-dozen locals sharing the cantina at the moment. A couple of them watched the trio's entrance. They gave them little notice or concern. Jack heard one simply dismiss them with the word *gringos*. As Jack saw the hate that seemed to go deep into the center man's eyes, he would have chosen the word *trouble*.

In all the times that Jack had moments like this, there was always a few seconds in which both sides would just stand and stare at one another. For most men, it took a little time to get their blood up. Few moments in a man's life would be this intense, as they waited for someone to make the first move. Not many could be calm in that sort of situation. Jack McCall always was.

During that brief time of face-off, Jack sized up the three hombres. They all wore their six-guns low, like they knew how to use them. Their right hands were held just above the pistol grip, like they intended to do just that. All three were covered in a thick layer of dust. They'd probably ridden long and hard to find him, Jack thought. The question of why puzzled him.

The angry man in the center, like the other two, was a stranger to Jack. Yet there was something familiar about him. He was tall, lean, and had a thin face. There was something about that face, but Jack couldn't put his finger on it.

The other two men did not show anger in their look or manner. Whereas the man between them obviously had a personal score to settle, these two seemed businesslike. Jack had faced enough hired guns to know the difference. Both men were of average height. The one on the left was a little older and a little heavier.

The tall man in the middle spoke first. His eyes were cold, angry, and fixed on Jack, but his words were directed at Dan. "You best clear out, old man!"

Dakota Dan moved just to Jack's left. He gave the tall "galoot" a wry smile. "Why would I want to do that, mister? I'd miss all the fun." He looked over to Jack and gave him a wink.

"Make the old fool listen to reason, Wes." The center man glanced toward the man standing to his right, but then resumed his hard stare at Jack.

Wes gave a couple nods. "Mister Foley, here," he gave the middle man a quick gesture with his left hand. "He's giving you a chance to live, old man. Now, drop your gunbelt and mosey. It's your partner we want." He made a little motion with his head toward the door. "Unless you want a gut full of lead, you better clear out now!" He said it in a matter-of-fact way, like he was doing Dan a favor.

Dan looked at the man called Wes and gave a terse shake of his head. "Ain't no bullets gonna be coming in this direction, sonny."

The man seemed genuinely puzzled by Dan's response and more than a little agitated with him. "This is your last chance, old man. You better take it while you can!"

Dan shook his head with some impatience. He looked at all three men as he spoke. "Maybe I should tell you what's about to happen here, since you three hombres are gonna miss most of it, on account of being dead."

They all gave him a condescending scowl, but he simply continued. "So, pretty soon, one of you tough galoots are gonna reach for your shootin' iron." Dan, enjoying his little oratory, smiled and gestured toward his partner. "That's when Jack here ventilates your carcasses and you drop to the floor."

The three men were seething now and quickly running out of patience, but Dan just kept talking. "As hot as it is, they'll probably drag the three of you out to the cemetery right away, before you start to stink." His eyebrows lowered some like he was giving the matter careful thought. "If I was writing your obituary it would say *three more men dumb enough to take on Diamondback McCall.*"

Foley's cold expression and focus on Jack remained unchanged. However, the two hired guns' faces went from agitation to surprise in an instant. Wes looked Jack up and down, giving him a careful study. "You really Jack McCall?"

He answered with a nod.

Wes slowly raised his hands to chest level, showing Jack his palms, and both men exchanged a nod of truce. "We been lied to, Jeb!" he stated angrily as he looked over to his partner standing to Foley's left.

The rage of Jeb was such that he immediately turned and gave Foley a hard shove. As Foley bumped into Wes and stumbled to a stop, Jeb lit into him. "A two-bit backshooter! An easy hundred dollars! Why, you lying varmint!" He put his right hand on his Colt. "If I shoot anybody, it's gonna be you!" His words came loud and fast.

Wes then gave Foley a push with his left hand, causing Foley to move back more and turn toward him. "A no-good bushwacking drifter, lookin' for a reputation! Ain't that what you told us?" he added with similar volume.

Foley, taken aback by this sudden turn of events, just stood there looking defeated. The anger was still there—Jack noted it simmering in those eyes—but his confidence was shaken.

Throughout the entire confrontation, Jack remained calm, to the point of appearing indifferent. He was alert, of course, but these men didn't require his absolute attention. Jack was way too fast for these three.

He liked Dan's handling of these men, and enjoyed the banter. He was also slightly amused by the outcome, but tried not to show it.

Wes moved back toward Jack McCall. He swallowed noticeably before he began. "Everybody knows you ain't like what Foley said, Mister McCall. And we know how fast you are." He glanced back over at his partner and then back to Jack. "You let us mosey, and you won't never see us again." He swallowed hard. "Got my word on it." He ended his little speech with a nod.

He sounded convincing alright, but on the other hand, he was a hired gun. Jack wasn't taking any chances. "You're free to go, the both of you. Just toss those six-shooters on the bar first."

Wes and Jeb looked to each other and then back at Jack. Jeb wore a blank expression. "What are we supposed to do without our guns?"

"You can live without them, or you can die with them. It's your call, boys." Jack put both hands over his two .45s, and loosened up his fingers for effect. He then gave the two nervous men a hard stare, leaving no doubt that he was serious. "What's it gonna be?"

The two men simply went to the bar, laid their hardware down, and turned for the door.

At that moment, Dan added, "Maybe you boys ought to consider another line of work."

They didn't even look back. As they headed out, Dan continued, but a little louder. "Can't remember ever seein' a hired gun much older than thirty!"

Shortly after they passed through the swinging doors, the sound of horse's hooves announced their departure. The locals decided to vacate now too. They had

been casually watching up to this point. Somehow they sensed it was no longer safe in there.

Dan smiled at his partner, who still had to deal with Foley. He stood a few steps away. That look of hate remained burning in his eyes. It was those eyes and something about his mouth that had seemed familiar, a family resemblance. Of course, when he first heard his name, it all made sense. Jack had only faced Foley's brother, Tex, for a few moments. But the face of a man you've killed stays with you.

Jack stepped a little closer to the latest Foley. Even without his two gunmen, he still looked ready to fight. His blood was up, and Jack knew it all too well. He looked into those seething eyes and spoke in a calm manner. "Revenge. That seldom goes the way you think it will, Foley." He noted his hand quivering a bit above his pistol, his teeth clenched. Now his words came louder and faster. "Your brother wanted a fight and now you do. What do I have to do, kill your whole family?!"

"Nobody could beat my brother in a fair fight! He was that good."

"That's what he thought, but it didn't work out that way."

"I say you bushwacked him, McCall! Everyone knows he was the fastest gun in Texas!"

"Then you should have told him."

"Told him what?"

"Told him to stay in Texas." Jack took two steps closer and stared into those angry eyes. "And you should have told him something else."

He just returned the stare.

"There's always somebody faster."

"If you're so fast, why do you need him?" Foley motioned toward Dan, who was enjoying the show.

"Don't give me a thought, mister." Dan shook his head and slowly pulled out his pistol, then tossed it onto the bar with his right hand. "I just want to watch." He smiled at both men and stepped away a little to his left.

"So, you just want a fair fight?"

He gave a quick nod and looked like he was ready to draw.

"Well, let's make sure it's fair. I don't want any other Foleys saying I bushwacked you." He said it with sarcasm while looking down at Foley's Colt. "So, why don't you put your hand on that pistol grip?"

Foley seemed a little tentative, but he did it.

"Now pull that shooter about halfway out, so you can get your finger on the trigger."

The Texan had a tinge of a smile as he did so.

"Might as well cock the thing too."

The hammer clicked as Foley poised to make his move. There was supreme confidence in those angry eyes.

"You're halfway there. I think that's fair enough." Jack stated with a calm voice, and just stood and waited.

Dan's eyes were very wide, his face seemed to be in shock. This wasn't something he expected.

Only a handful of seconds went by before Foley made his play. One gunshot rang out. As the deafening sound of the blast bounced off the adobe walls, Foley spun to his right and dropped his gun. He grabbed his forearm with his left hand and winced with pain. Blood flowed by his fingers, and a deep moan passed his lips.

Jack spun the smoking Colt in his right hand back into its holster, turned to Dan, and gave him a little smile.

Dan looked back at Jack and motioned toward the wounded Foley, "I don't know about his brother, but this feller's probably the slowest gun in Texas."

Foley, not appreciating the humor, spoke up through the pain, "I'm not slow."

"And your brother was fast." Jack stated as he walked up to the wounded Texan. "Just not fast enough."

"With your speed, why'd you have to kill him? You let me live."

"You said it yourself. He was that good. It was him or me."

He let his head drop a little, then looked back up at Jack. "That might be true, McCall, but you still killed my brother. That ain't something I can turn loose of." Although not quite as much, his eyes still retained their anger.

It might have been smart for Jack to have simply killed this man. There was always the chance that he'd come after him again later, and likely from behind. But Jack knew how this man felt. He'd been down the same trail of revenge. His father was backshot by three men, and nothing could have stopped him from taking vengeance. Foley's story, however, was different. He didn't have a just cause. Jack was betting that he had at least some sense of honor. "You've got yourself a problem, Foley." Jack gave him a couple nods. "Now you know I didn't bushwack your brother, but you've still got all that hate eating you up inside. And since you can't beat me in a fair fight, that leaves murder. I don't know about you, but I don't think your brother would be too proud of that."

Foley just looked away as Jack turned to the bartender, who was peeking over the bar. *"Donde esta un doctor, señor?"* he asked the frightened man.

The bartender stood up, looked toward the door, and then pointed to the right. *"Dos quadras a la izquierda, señor."*

Jack nodded while reaching into his pocket to settle the bar tab, adding, *"gracias."*

At that point, Foley just stood in the center of the room, staring at his bloody arm. He seemed dazed and lost. Jack walked over to him. "Best have that looked at. There's a doctor two blocks down on the left."

His eyes flicked up at Jack. "I know. I savvy Spanish."

Jack reached down and picked up Foley's gun. "I don't think you're the kind of man who'd come after me from behind. All the same, I'm keeping this."

He just turned away and headed out of the cantina.

As Jack watched Foley's departure, he suddenly noticed a familar face peering in one of the windows. It was Chota. His face was tense. He rushed to the entrance and bolted through the swinging doors.

Chapter 2
Greed

Chota rushed up to Jack and Dan. It was plain to see that he was troubled and also weary from a tough ride. He began speaking, but his voice sounded labored. "Jack, you must come back with me. There's trouble at village!"

Jack gave a little nod. "Slow down now, Chota. What's happened?"

Chota moved a little closer, like he wanted to be sure no one else would hear, and spoke softer. "You know lake you find in mountain?"

Jack nodded again.

"Two boys swim to dark side of lake. No one ever go dark side before. They not come back."

Jack's eyebrows lowered as he spoke. "When did this happen, and hasn't anybody tried to find them?"

"It happen early this morning." He gave Dan a quick glance, who looked as confused as his partner, and then continued. "Two older men went there to catch fish.

14

Boys go to swim. But now everyone is scared. They start thinking maybe Qualtari still there."

"Okay, Chota. I'll see to it. But I need to know something."

He gave a single nod.

"How long did it take to find us?"

"Not long, I see your horses right away."

"Well, did you see any riders coming from here when you rode in?"

He shook his head. "I see nobody 'til I get here."

Jack turned to Dakota Dan. "Looks like our two friends are still thinking about that hundred dollars."

He twisted his mouth as he thought of Wes and Jeb, and looked through the nearest arched window toward the street. "Dirty bushwackin' snakes. I bet they're hiding across the street right now, waiting for you to show yourself." He turned back to Jack. "What are you gonna do, partner?"

Jack looked around to his right, and focused on the door behind the bar. "Maybe it's time somebody bushwacked the bushwackers." Then he turned back toward his friends. "Chota, I'm sorry, but I've got a little unfinished business to settle first. Then we'll go after those boys. So, just sit down while I tend to this; you've had a long hard ride. Dan will tell you all about it."

"You don't need any help?" Dan knew the answer, but felt he should at least ask.

"Not this time." He went around the bar and opened the rear door. As he ducked down to go through the low doorway, he looked back at Dan. "This is kind of personal."

Jack had good reasons for going alone. However,

what he had just said was only part of it. Somebody trying to gun you down while lying in ambush is something anyone would consider personal. The fact that
they were breaking their word after he had let them go
didn't help either. But he also remembered the last time
Dan was involved with bushwackers. Jack wasn't going
to take a chance of him taking another bullet intended
for him.

He went up the street in the direction of the bootmaker's shop. He walked past the backside of it, knowing his ambushers were watching for his approach
nearby on the other side. Both his and Dan's horses
were tied in front of the *zapataria*. Wes and Jeb would
be waiting somewhere across the street.

Jack went two blocks up before heading right. Here,
he'd have to briefly be where he could be seen. The
street had to be crossed in order to get behind his rivals.
He knew that the two gunmen would be looking the
other way, toward the cantina. Still, he waited for an ox
cart he heard coming up from behind, got on its left
side, ducked down, and crossed with it. There was no
point in tipping his hand.

When he rounded the street that ran back in the same
direction as the cantina, but more importantly behind
the bushwackers, he saw their horses. A little over a
block and a half down were two cowponies tied to a
post. They carried Western saddles and bridles. As Jack
got closer, he noted each had long leather sheaths attached to the front of the saddles. They were intended
to carry a rifle. They were both empty.

Just ahead of the horses was an alley. Jack approached it slowly and carefully. His eyes scanned all directions as he moved his head around the corner of the adobe building for a look.

The alley was the length of two buildings and barely wide enough to allow a wagon to pass through. The buildings on each side were made of decaying brick and adobe. The walls went up in a typically Spanish fashion to a straight and level edge. Round, wooden poles protruded in a line near the top. They supported the unseen roof, which rested flat atop the walls. This sort of architecture always reminded Jack more of a fort than a business or dwelling.

At the end of the alley, on the left side, was Wes. He was kneeling down in a crouch, peering around the corner. His rifle was held in both hands and pointed toward the cantina.

Jack quietly moved along the right-hand wall until he was over halfway down the length of the alley. He kept his back to the wall. Positioning himself this way, he couldn't be backshot. It also gave him a commanding field of view. If anybody suddenly appeared, he'd see them, and if Jack McCall could see them, there was little question of who would come out on top.

Jack couldn't see Jeb at the moment, but he had a pretty good idea of where he was. Jack looked down at Wes, several steps away, and spoke in an almost off-handed way. "Looking for me?"

Wes spun around while raising the rifle skyward with his right hand. He was off balance and wore an expression of pure shock.

Jack motioned with his right hand for him to stand.

As he got to his feet, Jack gave him a cold stare. "Where's your partner?"

It seemed to take some effort on his part to get any words out at all. Even then, they sounded unconvincing. "Ah . . . he left. He went north, Mr. McCall." There was an uneasy waver in the tone.

"North, huh? Seems like he would have made better time if he rode his horse."

Wes just stood there nervously, still holding the rifle and aiming it upward. The fact that he had just been caught in a lie had no effect on his expression.

"I seem to remember something about you giving me your word back at the cantina. Somehow when you said I'd never see you again, I didn't think this was what you meant." He gave the frightened gunman a look of disgust. "I guess you were right, though; I wouldn't have seen you if you shot me from behind this building." The corners of Jack's mouth went down, leaving no doubt of what he thought of him. "So I suppose you weren't actually lying. Of course, it also means you're a no-good bushwacking coward!"

Wes could see that Jack was deadly serious, yet his eyes kept looking up and around. There was no question that he was scared, but his attention was not entirely on the man before him.

Jack noticed the eye movement of his foe. It was no surprise. He stayed watchful for Jeb's appearance and continued with Wes. "When I got here, you wanted to point that Winchester in my direction." His frown curled up into a slight smile. "Why don't you try it now?"

"I got no chance against you."

Jack could hear some movement above on the building he was facing. He kept equally alert to that as he answered. "So maybe you think I should let you go?"

He returned a surprised nod.

Jack noted the barrel of a Winchester being eased over the top edge of the wall. "Yeah, I'll let you go." He stated, while noting Wes flick his eyes up at the same rifle. "I'll let both of you go," he braced for action and stated coldly, "straight to the devil's inferno!"

They both made their move on Jack at the very same time. Wes swung the rifle down as Jeb raised up from atop the roof to take aim. Jack drew both .45s at once. His right hand went for Jeb on the roof. The left hand crossed under his right for Wes. Two shots were fired, yet it sounded like only one very loud bang.

Wes and Jeb had been partners. They had ridden together and shared the same trail of violence. They died in the same instant and shared one more thing. They each had a bullet between their eyes. Such was the inevitable end of their lives. Such was the price of greed. Such was the code of the West.

Jeb's head and arms hung over the edge of the wall with the rifle still in his right hand. It soon fell to the ground. Jack picked it up, went over to Wes, who was lying on his back, and took the Winchester that laid beside him. The spoils of war, so to speak. Anyway, Dan and Chota could use these weapons. Wes and Jeb certainly needed them no more.

Jack did not linger long. He had no choice in this grim affair, and wasn't about to brood over it. He was needed elsewhere and knew if the Mexican authorities got involved, he would lose valuable time.

Within minutes he had gathered his two amigos, collected Dan's boots, and headed out into the desert. It would take several hours to reach Spirit Feather. A long ride on a hot day. Jack hoped he would reach the village in time, and wondered what awaited him there in the darkness.

Chapter 3
Into the Depths

Had Jack not been in such a hurry to leave Nogales, he would have picked up a few more things that might have come in handy. Still, he knew it would be foolish to go into the depths without some pretty long ropes. Jack figured the rope that he always carried over his saddle horn would most likely be useless. It was a special rope for doing tricks and was very short. He kept it merely as a sentimental reminder of his days with the Western carnival. So while Dan settled up with the bootmaker, Jack went a few stores down and bought a couple fifty-foot lengths of rope. During the long ride, he tied one into a lasso. Other than those two ropes, all he brought along were a couple knives and his wits. Of course, Chota had seen to some torches and matches.

It took over three hours to ride across the parched desert toward the mountain with the two spires. The heat made for a difficult trip for both man and horse. Time was important. All that was known was that the two boys had disappeared. Whether or not it was too late was something no one wanted to consider.

It was late afternoon by the time the threesome reached the hidden village. The rope ladder was still in place at the entrance to the underground lake. They wasted little time in climbing up the mountain to that point.

Jack had to decide whether to go it alone again. He thought back to the last time he ventured into the dark unknown of the caverns within this mountain. It was one of the most physically demanding exploits he had ever been involved in. Although always willing, Dan was a little too old. Chota simply wasn't a particularly strong man. Jack was there to save two young boys; he didn't need to be rescuing his friends, too.

When they reached the rocks surrounding the small opening in the ground that was the entrance to the underground lake, Jack bid his friends adios. They accepted his going alone without explanation. They each shook his hand and wished him luck. Jack was going off to face unknown danger again. This sort of farewell was just a part of being Jack's friend. They would go back down the mountain and wait and worry inside the hidden city.

Guns were useless where he was going, as were his hat and boots. He handed them to Dan before his two friends left. He had the two knives attached to his belt. Both ropes were looped around his neck. The two torches were tucked into his pants, with the matches in his mouth. Jack had doubts about the usefulness of the torches. He didn't need them at first; there was enough light coming in from the cavern entrance and a few other small openings on that side of the lake. Where he was going, however, was the dark area of the lake. Whether to light a torch right away or save them was on his mind. Still, if he found those boys hurt, he would need light to tend to them. *The safe bet,* he thought, *was not to use them up too soon.* The other problem was keeping the torches dry while in the water. He didn't know where he would be going, but he would have to swim to get there.

He descended the forty-some feet of rope ladder quickly, this time ignoring the vein of gold that caused him so much trouble during his escape from this place. The cavern was just as he remembered. The light streaming in from above glistened off the calm, clear water. The roof of the cavern still reminded him of a cathedral. Large fish could be seen from time to time. He glanced down to see if there were bubbles coming up from the geyser that he rode to freedom the last time he was there. He saw none.

As he entered the water, he took the two torches out from his waist and held them in his left hand. He then held them up out of the water while swimming on his back. As he swam, it became ever darker. The light at the entrance grew dim and was becoming smaller. This part of the lake was new to Jack and where he was going was a mystery. Taking risks and accepting challenges were nothing new to him. Danger was a part of his life. In fact, that was when he was at his best.

Because of the darkness, it was impossible for Jack to judge the size of the lake. It was bigger than he would have guessed, just from the distance he had traveled. Still, he could see nothing from side to side. His means of navigation was very simple. Although his eyes at this time were of no use to him, he was able to hear something. Other than the sound of running water ahead of him, it was eerily quiet. He slowly swam along—still on his back—toward that sound, which reminded him of a brook.

Time goes slowly in total darkness. It had probably been no more than ten minutes since Jack first entered the water, but he would have guessed that it was much longer than that.

Jack now noticed a couple things. There was suddenly a little current and he tipped his head back in the direction he was going. Soon, he knew he was nearing the end of the lake, for he could just make out the approaching cavern wall. What fascinated him most was an opening in the cavern wall and the dim greenish glow coming from it.

It was a most curious sight: a rugged opening right at water level, looking like a small tunnel entrance. It occurred to Jack that the green light would have likely lured those two boys toward it. He figured he was probably going in the right direction.

The water then began making a rushing sound and at the same time the speed of the current started to pick up. Jack found himself being pulled along with the current into the opening, wishing he wasn't on his back. Feeling out of control, he dropped the torches, spit out the matches, and spun around to face the direction in which he was being carried along. He was suddenly moving much faster.

The lake's bottom angled downward at that point,

and within a second or two, he was already inside the tunnel-like opening in the cavern wall. The tunnel wasn't very long; he could just make that out from the faint emerald glow that appeared slightly brighter ahead. Jack frantically extended his hands and feet against the sides of the five-foot-wide opening in an effort to slow down, but it didn't work. It wasn't that there was a lot of water flowing down. The problem was that everything was so slippery. The steep angle, and the fact that he was going so fast, didn't help either. Desperately he pushed harder in an effort to gain control of the descent, then suddenly, there was nothing beneath him.

Jack fell downward into an empty space colored with that strange green tint. As he fell, he concluded that he was in some sort of vertical shaft. He didn't know what might be at the bottom. It could be water; it could be rock. If it was rock, he had to move fast. He pulled the top rope from around his neck, opened up a loop, and hurled it out against the side of the shaft. It would have been pure luck if it worked. It didn't.

Just before he hit, Jack noticed an opening on one side of the shaft. The light was brighter there, but he was falling so fast that he caught but a glimpse of the greenish-lit cavity.

He hit feet first. The water was very hot and, fortunately, very deep. As he plunged deep into the black and scorching hot pool, a burning pain swept over him and he immediately felt weak. He didn't even try to swim up, but simply let himself float to the surface.

It took a little time for Jack to get his breath. There was a spray of water coming down from above. That helped a little, but he knew that he couldn't last long where he was. The pain was something that he could deal with. He was a tough guy, but he could feel his strength slipping away. That sort of heat would cause him to pass out soon. Whatever he did, he had to do it quick.

The vertical shaft that Jack found himself in went straight up and was fairly wide. Above him was the cavity he saw just before he hit the water. It was a little more than his six feet up to the cavity's floor. That was the origin of the light, the greenish hue that spread across the shaft. Although you certainly couldn't call it a bright light, it was enough to make out the general shape and some detail. High above, and Jack calculated that to be nearly the length of both his ropes, was the lake. That was the source of the water descending on him and the point from which he fell. It was not of particular interest to him at the moment. He had to find a way out of the hot water.

The walls of the shaft had a glassy feel, almost like it was polished. It was so smooth and slick that scaling it was out of the question. He guessed that the shaft was created by volcanic activity, probably advancing and retreating lava. That would explain why it was so smooth, but it wasn't getting him any closer to that cavity above him.

In spite of falling a great distance into extremely hot water, Jack had somehow managed to hang on to the rope he had used earlier. The only thing he could think of was to simply toss the lasso up into the cavity and hope it caught something.

Just as he started to wind it up for his first attempt, he felt the water begin to churn. Rushing bubbles and steam started flooding up, and with it, even hotter water. But at the same time, the pool began to rise. Jack had heard of pools that rose and fell from a heat source deep beneath it. None of that mattered to him, though. He was coming up to the cavity above, and none too soon. As the water lifted him up, the temperature was becoming agonizing. Jack slipped the rope back around his neck and mustered all his strength and will. When the water level got within a foot of the cavity floor, he reached up, and began pulling himself up. He managed to swing his left leg up and over the edge, and from there, pulled and rolled onto a fairly flat rock floor. He turned over on his back, laid there motionless, and let out a heavy sigh. As he closed his eyes, there was a sudden rustling sound to his right. He turned his head to see the two young boys coming toward him. He smiled briefly and noted that they seemed alright. Then his mind and vision blurred, and he drifted into a deep sleep.

Jack didn't know how long he had been unconscious. He sat up and let his senses come around. Even in the misty green glow, he could see that his skin was quite red. It seemed that every part of his body had a stinging, burning sensation. Yet, aside from that and feeling unusually tired, he felt good enough to start figuring a way out of the place.

As his vision cleared and ajusted to the green light, he studied the cavity that he had ended up in. It was a very strange place. The cavity itself was roughly oval shaped. It was the same width as the vertical shaft and quite high. It grew smaller the deeper it went, ending in crumbled boulders and debris, some forty-odd feet back. It was apparent that the relatively small cavity was once part of a larger cavern, the rest having collapsed long ago. Jack also noticed that the bottom layer of the boulders was wet. Obviously that rising pool occasionally spilled into the cavity, the water escaping through the rocks.

What made the place so strange were the pools, steam vents, and a number of rock columns. Throughout the floor of the chamber were numerous phosphorescent pools and small holes where steam escaped. The bubbling pools gave off the green light, a chemical reaction that Jack had never seen. Between the steam spewing up and the flickering streams of green- and aqua-colored light, it made for a ghostly image of swirling gray shadows and twisting greenish hues.

The two boys were huddled together behind Jack. They were understandably frightened and weary from their ordeal, but otherwise looked better off than Jack. Their skin was not so affected by the hot water. Jack did not know their language, but it was easy to figure why the boys came out so well—a simple matter of timing. The pool was rising and falling in about six-minute intervals. The boys were lucky enough to hit the water when it was at or near the top, so they got out fast, with less time exposed to the heat.

He smiled at the two young boys, and they smiled right back. They were probably only eight- to ten-years old, he thought. He knew that if he was going to be of any use to them, he had to think of something fast. Time was not on his side. He was only going to get weaker.

Jack got to his feet. He would have liked to say that

he'd felt worse before, but it wouldn't be true. As he gazed up into the shaft for some means of escape, he saw little that was encouraging. It was a long way up, with the same smooth rock except for at the very top. Just above the tunnel-like opening to the lake, where water flowed into shaft, there were protrusions of rough and jagged-looking rocks. The light was poor that far up, but he could make out that much. It looked like a large chunk of rock had broken off and fallen down the shaft, leaving the jagged remains. That was the only promising thing he saw; yet, he didn't know how to make use of it. Even on a good day, he couldn't throw a rope that high straight up. And he wasn't having a good day.

Jack took another look around the steamy, green chamber. It felt like a Turkish bathhouse, and as the sweat ran down his tender skin, it stung even more. Still, Jack always thought with calculating logic, and as he studied the formations and features through the thick atmosphere, he started to get an idea.

Beside the pools and steam vents, Jack took notice of the vertical stalactites and stalagmites. This place had been a closed cavern at some point in the past, and these icicle- and cone-shaped columns were formed over the ages. Jack's attention was then drawn to a particular steam vent that was quite near the vertical shaft. It was nearly round and spewed hot vapor up into the shaft.

An idea started to take shape in Jack's mind. A desperate long shot, but he could think of nothing else. He was going to try to use the power of steam and the weight of a tapered stone to propel his rope up to that rocky spot above the lake entrance.

He noted the size and shape of that steam vent and

then headed toward the cluster of various rock columns. Once he found the right-sized stone to force into that steam vent, he had to use his knife to chisel and break it off. Next, he had to securely attach one end of the rope to the stone, drive the tapered end of the stone hard into the steam vent, and wait. While he waited for the pressure to build, he tied the other rope to the end of the first one. It was a long way up, and both ropes would just about do it. He then coiled up the rope beside the steam vent, held on to the end of rope, and stood back.

It took a while, maybe eight or ten minutes. When it finally blew, it went with a sudden blast, followed by a very loud and high-pitched roar. The stone soared high up into the shaft like a Fourth of July rocket. It came down like a rock. Jack pulled the projectile out of the searing water and tried again. In fact, it took eleven tries before it lodged into those jagged rocks above.

Jack tugged hard on the rope. It seemed secure. Next, he looped and tied the end of the rope just under the arms of each of the boys and left a five-foot length between them. He gave the two lads a reassuring smile, rubbed the top of their heads for good luck, and started up.

It wasn't going to be easy—Jack found that out right away. It wasn't just the distance he had to climb, it was also the water. As it cascaded down, the water made the rope slick and the walls so slippery that he wasn't able to use his feet against them in the ascent. Even under normal circumstances this would be a very tough climb. As it was, in a weakened condition and with hands that were already burned, he would be going on sheer will.

The wet rope required a two-handed grip to pull himself up. Using both feet, Jack twirled the rope around his right foot, held it in place with his left foot, and then reached up for the next grip. It was slow and painful, but it was working. Jack found himself breathing hard. The pain in his palms grew worse. It took a powerful grip against the slick rope each time he pulled himself up, and as he got more tired, his grip began slipping. As time and the climbing went on, his hands became raw. The rope was now stained with blood.

As he climbed ever higher and finally neared the opening that led back to the lake and cavern, he noted another obstacle. The steam projectile lodged into the jagged rocks was not only a ways above the opening, it was also off to the left side of it. The rope hung several feet beside the tunnel-like opening, and Jack could now see that it was the only way back into the lake. He also saw that in order to get into the opening and back into the lake, he would have to position himself beside it and start a swinging motion to hurl himself into it.

Jack lined himself up with the opening. He glanced down at the two boys. They had been watching the whole climb from the edge of the chamber. He twirled the rope around his right foot and ankle, and then started pushing off with his left foot. It was obvious that he had to have enough momentum. He needed to get beyond the slippery, angled section. He pushed off harder, and each time he would come out farther. When he was getting about a six-foot arc, he pushed off hard and to the right.

He knew it wouldn't work if he went in feet first. He would need his hands for any chance of finding a grip. So as he swung forward and into the opening, he pushed off with the rope to get his feet behind him. Then he let go of the rope with his hands and lunged in, headfirst. He desperately reached out with both hands in an effort to find something to get hold of. As he hit hard on his chest, he bounced and momentarily stopped. He started sliding back. Just as before he pushed out with his hands, but he continued to slip back. Within a second he felt his feet go over the edge and on he went until the last contact with his fingertips. He fell downward. Suddenly the rope took hold. As the weight of his body pulled against the rope wound around his right leg, it started slipping. The rope first slipped off his foot. Jack began going down again. The coiled rope was turning around his leg and causing a rope burn on top of his already-seared skin. The few remaining coils started coming off, one after the other. Jack was hanging upside down by his ankle, but he knew in just a moment he'd be in a free-fall. He quickly grabbed the rope as it trailed beneath him and started wrapping it around his left wrist. Just as he put the rope inside the grip of his left hand, his ankle came free. His feet came around and then his whole weight hit home on that wrist.

For several minutes, Jack just hung there. He looked up at the opening and shook his head. If there was another way, he would gladly try it but there wasn't. He took a deep breath and started up again.

It took a little while before he was ready to give it another try. As Jack stared at the opening again, he remembered something that his mother had taught him as a boy. It was how to roll and tumble.

With that in mind, he pulled a little slack in the rope from below and then held the rope at his waist with his right hand. Then he started bouncing off the wall next to the opening. He once again got the arc up to six feet and pushed off for all he was worth. When he came forward into the tunnel-like opening, he released the rope, got into a tucked position, and rolled on up the angled/tunnel floor. This got him several feet farther than the time previous and beyond the tilt. He then immediatly flattened out and reached down. Once he got his hand behind a protruding rock below the shallow waterline, he was then able to pull himself ahead until he found a secure foothold.

Now it was time to pull up the boys. They probably weighed no more than a hundred and fifty pounds together. Not much for a man like Jack McCall, but considering his condition and what he had just gone through, he wasn't looking forward to it. He took another deep breath, clenched his teeth, and got on with it.

Chapter 4
The Golden Idol

A dim reddish glow cast through the doorway and window of the small adobe room. Jack's eyes started adjusting to the light and his mind began to emerge from a long sleep. His senses were dulled, and it took some time to come around. As he tried to sit up, he felt the pain return. Most of the muscles of his body ached. The stinging, burning sensation of his skin abruptly brought him back to reality.

He pushed down harder with his thickly bandaged hands and managed to sit up straight. He found himself breathing heavily from the effort. He looked around the small stark room. Other than a pitcher and bowl beside the mat that he lay on, it seemed empty. As he tried to make sense of his surroundings, he heard a familiar voice behind him from the doorway. "You had me worried sweetheart," Fawn's soft words were tinged with concern.

The pain seemed to fade a little as he turned to see

her lovely face. A smile replaced the grimace that was there just a moment before. She knelt beside him and kissed him gently. He took her hand, and for nearly a minute, fell captive to her beautiful dark eyes. His eyes finally moved from side to side, then back to hers. "How did I get here?"

"You were carried here, unconscious." She gave a little nod.

"I don't remember much. It's all kind of hazy."

"Well, the two boys told me what you went through down there. They also said that after you pulled them up to the lake, you looked pretty bad. I guess you managed to get up the rope ladder all right, but when you started down the hill, you passed out. They went for help and got a couple men to bring you back here to the village."

"Are the boys all right?"

"They're fine."

"How long have I been out?"

"A whole day. When Chota couldn't wake you up, he came after me. You got everybody pretty scared. Chota thought maybe I could help."

"So, you've been doing a little nursing?"

She ran her finger along his bare shoulder and turned her fingertip up before his eyes. "There wasn't much that we could do, except to rub this aloe over your burned skin."

It was the first time he had noticed that his body was covered with greenish gel. In fact, it was only then that he realized that other than the blanket, he was wearing nothing. He suddenly felt rather embarrassed and looked her way shyly. "So who took off my clothes and covered me in this stuff?"

"I did."

Now he was really embarrassed.

She was trying hard not to giggle. "I'm teasing. It was done before I got here. Chota took care of that. All I could do was to keep a damp cloth on your forehead until the fever broke a while ago."

His face displayed a certain amount of relief, while managing a little smile.

She simply smiled back. Then she reached down and poured some water from the pitcher into the small bowl and put it to his lips. "You've got to drink as much water as you can. You lost a lot when you got overheated."

He let her tilt the bowl and drank it all.

"I'm going to get you some food now, okay?"

He nodded.

She kissed him lightly again and then whispered into his ear, "I can't let you go off on these adventures of yours again, not knowing if you're coming back or not." She stood up and started for the doorway, then looked back. "From now on, I'm going with you." She ended it with a firm nod before leaving. Jack watched Fawn's exit, her white cotton dress clinging just enough to reveal every curve. He was able to smile through the pain.

Within a few minutes, she returned with the food. It took a little coaxing, but he finished the simple meal of rabbit, beans, and tortillas. Jack was still quite weak and was soon back to sleep. He did a lot of sleeping during the next week. Then on the eighth day, he seemed to come out of his state of fatigue. He felt and looked much better. His skin was still rather red and several layers had peeled off by then, but he was in good spirits. He moved to his usual quarters, a large dwelling that the chief designated for Jack and his friends. The small room he had been in was chosen because it was away from the noisy routine of the village. They knew he needed a quiet place to rest, but now he appreciated the company. The people of the village had already held Jack in high esteem. After this last episode, they viewed him with even greater respect. The fact that he had saved two children was part of it. The way he would willingly go into places that they feared was another. Perhaps what they found most endearing was that he would go through so much for them.

Jack was always greeted with smiles and fond expressions as he wandered through the city. He would also find himself often being followed by some of the smaller children. He not only felt comfortable with these people, he felt at home with them. He had not yet learned the language, yet he had a sense of belonging, like he was one of them. There was also a sense of respect on Jack's part. It wasn't just that he found these people warm, genuine, and honest, but he really admired their talent and ingenuity. To build a city like this one was a monumental task. It required exceptional people. They worked for generations constructing the complex that terraced up into the cavern walls. When he gazed up at the stone and adobe buildings, one upon the other and sometimes five stories high, he was always impressed. When he considered that they had only crude tools and masonry skills, he found it amazing.

Early the next morning he was having the usual corn, beans, and tortilla breakfast with Dan and Fawn. As was his custom, Chota came in to join them. Jack noticed that he seemed to have something on his mind, and he soon chose to share it. "I talk to chief. He want talk to you, Jack."

"What's on his mind, Chota?"

"He not tell me. He just say come see him."

"Can it wait until after breakfast?"

Chota nodded while Dan and Fawn exchanged puzzled expressions.

Fawn knew it was a struggle for Chota to interpret the chief's words in English. He was far more at home with her native language. She looked over to him. "Do I need to translate, like the last time?"

"That good idea," he answered while noticing that Dan was looking rather left out. "You come too, Dan. Chief won't mind."

The corners of Dakota Dan's mouth instantly turned up.

With anxious curiosity, they finished breakfast in minutes. Chota then led the way across the courtyard, by the fountain and up the steps of the Kiva. Then they descended the stairway that led them to the ceremonial chamber.

There were several torches lit around the circular room. The chief sat near the center on a thick mat. It seemed obvious that he had been waiting for them. He looked up at Jack and gave a little smile. With a quick sweep of his right hand, Tecanay motioned for his guests to sit. Chota sat to the chief's left with Fawn beside him. Jack and Dan huddled close to Fawn so she wouldn't have to talk above the chief. There were enough ocotillo mats placed around the village leader so that no one had to sit on stone.

As Tecanay began speaking, Chota would relay it to
Fawn in Papago, she would then quietly tell it in English. Tecanay directed his gaze and words toward Jack.
"We believe that the spirits have sent you to help our
people. For this we thank the spirit world and you." He
gave Jack a nod of appreciation and it was returned.
The chief's face then seemed to become more serious.
Jack sensed that he was about to get to the real purpose
of the meeting.

"I told you once of how we were driven away from
our city in the canyon by the Apache. And how, long
before we came to live down here, there were many
more of us. In those early days, the harvest was good
and we would trade with other tribes. From other tribes
we heard of a great city far to the south by the blue water. They said it was a place of temples and gold and
our chief sent three men to find it. They traveled along
the southern river to the blue water. They followed the
blue water for many days until they came upon a land
that was thick with trees and filled with strange animals. Then, finally, they saw tall temples and beautiful
stone buildings. It was one of the great Aztec cities, and
the Aztec people welcomed our men. They also taught
them many things. The way we build with stone, our
way of farming, and even the ways of the spirit world
we learned from them." He stopped for just a few seconds so that he and his interpreters could take a breath.
He then continued. "There was something else that
they gave to us and it was presented to our people by an
Aztec priest. It was a hawk, a golden hawk, and you
know that we believe the hawk to be from the spirit
world. This golden idol was cherished by our people

for many generations. But then there was the time of the Apache raids. We knew it had to be hidden before the Apache stole it." Tecanay took another little breath and smiled at Jack. "Will you find it and bring it back to us?"

Jack looked both surprised and confused. "You don't know where it was hidden?"

Tecanay listened to Chota relay the question and nodded. "In a cave below the great river." With confusion now on the face of all but the chief, he reached behind and picked up a rolled leather scroll. He then passed it along to Jack.

After carefully unrolling the fragile and ancient script, Jack briefly studied what was some sort of map. He then handed it to Fawn, while adding, "Looks like the Grand Canyon to me."

She looked it over and nodded in agreement. Her eyes narrowed as she turned to Chota. "Ask the chief what he means by below the river."

Chota asked her question and the chief began telling the story. Again the interpreters relayed his words. "There was a time when the rains did not come. After three dry years even the great river was only a stream. The great canyon was always a sacred place for us. Our people would go there to pray to the spirits. They ask spirits how to keep idol away from Apache. Then they see a place. Because the river was so low, they see a small cave, just above the water, in the canyon wall. They believe this is a sign. So they hide the golden hawk inside cave. They know Apache never go down into canyon, so idol is safe. Then, later, after we find this place and start to build a new city, we send men to bring idol back here. But then the rains had come again, and river not let them back inside." He looked at Jack sincerely. "That was long ago, but I think you can find it. Golden hawk waits for you. Will you bring it back to us?"

Jack held up one finger and turned to his Indian friend. "Ask him one thing, Chota. Wouldn't the river have washed that statue out of that cave?"

Chota asked the question.

He shook his head. "The cave goes in and then up. The idol was placed very high on a rock ledge."

Jack smiled at Fawn, who had doubt all over her face. "You still want to go on one of my adventures?"

"You really think there's any chance of finding it?"

"You know me. I can't resist a challenge."

She smiled, "Well, I always wanted to see the Grand Canyon."

Chapter 5
A Very Long Ride

As Jack continued to recover over the next few days, he had time to think and to study the old map. It seemed plain enough that he could get close to where the idol was hidden. He was pretty sure that the section of the Grand Canyon on the map was just north of Red Butte. It was relatively easy to determine that from the creeks, rivers, passes, and mountains leading to that point. The map also had pictographs and some strange symbols at the very spot where the cave was supposed to be that Jack couldn't figure out. One in particular, was a *V*-shaped marking below and to the right of what might be described as a flat mushroom. Then between the *V* was what looked like a lightening bolt. Below those symbols were markings resembling a letter *L* and an hourglass, both lying on their side. So the question of whether he could actually find a cave beneath the river remained doubtful. To then enter and retrieve the statue seemed a real longshot. However, there was little

that could discourage Jack McCall from taking on a challenge. He had also given the chief a promise to go after the golden hawk and that was just what he would do. Still, as he pondered the distance to the Grand Canyon, there was no getting around the fact that this was going to be a very long ride.

Jack knew that Dan would ride along. He was his partner and that was simply understood. What Jack wasn't so sure about was Fawn's insistence on going too. One of the many things he liked about her was her spirit and self-confidence. Now that independence meant she would be making a physically grueling trek. They would be riding through the searing heat of the desert and negotiating some tough mountain passes. Of course, he knew that she was of sturdy stock and had grown up on horseback. So his concerns were not strictly realistic. The fact of the matter was that he loved her. She was the only girl that he had ever felt this way about and he wanted to protect her. But she had made her position clear. She was going.

When they left the hidden city to begin the journey, it was about two hours before sunup and still quite dark. After walking their horses in the gully that crossed the canyon entrance for nearly half a mile, they mounted up and headed for the Papago village. It had become a simple matter of routine. No one would find the entrance to the city by a careless shortcut. Leaving in darkness and staying out of sight in the gully assured that.

They rode on as the sun rose over their right shoulders. The miles went by and the temperature climbed. The rugged desert stretched out before them with a variety of cactus in every direction. There wasn't a single

cloud in the sky and not a breath of wind. It was un-
comfortably warm already, but nothing like it would be
in the afternoon. Yet, Jack's two companions didn't
seem to mind. Dan was obviously glad to be going
along on another adventure. Jack could see that in his
expression. He wore a boyish smile and there was a
glint in his eyes. Fawn also seemed happy to be by
Jack's side. Although she surely felt the same way
about him as he did about her, he sensed it was more
than that. Not many women got to go off on crazy adventures. This was exciting for her.

The hours passed slowly, and they finally rode by the
mission and over to the area where the Papagos did
business. They were happy to step down off their
horses and find some shade. It was midday and very
hot. After drinking a considerable amount of water and
cooling down by a large mesquite, each briefly went
their separate ways.

Dan's primary interest, as usual, was to order up
some vittles. Fawn had people to see. She had many
friends at the village, not the least of which were the
children she had been teaching. Without giving the
real reason for her trip, she told them that she would
be back soon and gave the kids a hug. Jack had to see
to the horses and supplies. He spotted the young boy
that usually tended to horses and made a deal, knowing that they were in good hands. Then, while buying
the meat, beans, corn flour, and grain for the horses,
he happened to notice that some of the women were
carrying water in animal-skin bags. They were made
from a goat's stomach and tapered down to a small
wooden spout. He got the attention of a woman carry-

ing one of the balloon-shaped water bags and offered her two dollars for it. She was more than happy to make the sale.

This was only the first stop of a long, tough ride that would test both horses and riders. They spent the night at the Papago village and then headed northwest the next morning. They had to carry enough water and supplies for three days. That took them to the Pima and Maricopa Indian reservation. There they stopped again for supplies.

After six days the terrain had gone from desert to red rock mountains with trees replacing the cactuses. It was higher and a little cooler, but not much.

Jack preferred to get supplies from local Indians instead of going into towns. There was always a risk involved when he did so. He thought of all the times he had been challenged by some young gunhand looking for a reputation. With Jack's speed, the risk was not of being shot, but rather that he'd be forced into a gunfight. He wanted no part in a killing, but he would defend himself if it came to that. With Dan and Fawn along, it was more risky. He didn't want bullets intended for him going their way.

They would have to go into the next town; however, they needed supplies and the reservations were all to the south. It was nearly noon when they rode into Prescott, a large and very busy city.

Dust was continually kicked up from the many hooves and wheels moving along the crowded and powder-dry streets. There was the sound, the jumbled throng that makes a city seem alive. An odd mixture of noises. A chorus of voices, music, laughter, and the horses and wagons in the streets all at once. Jack thought it a stark contrast from the still quiet on the trail of the last few days.

It was Jack's intention to make this a quick stop. Just in the first minute or so since they entered the business district he noticed several gunhands. They were easy to spot. There was a look about them. It wasn't just their hardware. Jack could see it in the way they moved, the way they dressed, and in the cold, hard expression on their faces. They usually congregated around saloons or just lingered along the boardwalk, looking for trouble. Towns had a way of drawing gunmen and trouble like a magnet.

Dan and Fawn rode to each side of Jack as they busied themselves looking at the people and storefronts, trying to find a mercantile store. As Jack turned his head, he noticed that Fawn's horse was walking with a slight limp. He pointed down toward the animal's left front hoof, which looked to have a loose shoe.

She returned a nod. "It must have happened a little ways back. I felt him stumble on a rock."

"That will have to be seen to while we're here," Jack added.

Dan then motioned ahead with his right hand. "Seems like I remember a blacksmith at the end of this street from the last time I was in these parts."

They rode on, and just like Dan thought, there was a stable and blacksmith at the very end of town on the right-hand side. The stable was more prominent. It was a large unpainted barn with Meyers Livery over the open double doors. Attached around the right side was the blacksmith's shop. It was simply a lean-to over a hearth, water trough, anvil, and sundry tools of the trade.

When they reached the blacksmith's shop, the burly smithy was sitting on a small stool affixing a shoe to the left rear hoof of a chestnut mare. Jack noted the sweat flowing from his forehead and didn't envy his occupation, especially in the heat of an Arizona summer.

All three dismounted and tied their horses to the hitching rail that stretched from the right side of the stable doorway all the way to the blacksmith's shop, nearly twenty feet. Jack walked over to the smithy's right side with Fawn and Dan just behind him.

Having noted potential customers, he set the horse's hoof down easy and turned toward Jack. "How can I help you folks?" His unshaven face glistened with perspiration and his dirty plaid shirt was soaked with sweat, but he managed a pleasant enough smile.

"Got a loose shoe on that bay," Jack motioned toward Fawn's mount. "When do you think you could tend to it?"

"That wouldn't take long. I'll work it in just as soon as I finish up this one."

"Good enough," Jack nodded. "Could you steer me to the nearest mercantile hereabouts? We're short on supplies."

"Sure thing, mister." He pointed across the front of the stable, down the left side of the street. "You hear that noise? A whole lot of loud voices and that tinny sounding piano down there?"

Jack nodded.

"Well, just before you get to that noisy saloon there's Buckman's General Store. He can fix you up."

"Much obliged." Jack gave a single nod and turned back to Dan and Fawn. "So who's going with me?"

Dan gestured toward the stable doorway. "While you're gettin' the grub, I thought maybe I'd go in here and see about some grain for the ponies. Thought they'd probably have some tack for sale too. My cinch strap's cracked and that worries me a mite."

"Better see to it, Dan." He watched his partner head into the stable and then looked over to Fawn and smiled. "You coming?"

Her eyes moved in the direction of the boisterous saloon and then back to his. "Maybe I should stay here and watch the horses."

Jack could see that she sensed trouble down that street, yet he didn't like leaving her either. Before Jack had time to consider what would be the safe move, the smithy turned around and spoke up. "It might not be my place to say it, mister, but bad things happen around that saloon. Nothing but drunks and gunhands will go near the place. If any of that lot see her, well . . . it won't be pretty." He had the face of a man you could trust, and he certainly knew the town better than any of them.

Jack found himself nodding at the big man in agreement. He then went to Fawn and gave her a little kiss. "You're right. Just keep an eye on the horses 'til I get back. I'll make it quick."

She smiled and gave him a hug.

He then headed for the store. This was the end of

town and there were only buildings on the left side. Jack crossed over and walked along the boardwalk. The farther he went, the louder the noise from the saloon. As he passed the first three stores—a Chinese laundry, a druggist, and a dentist's office—he noticed that there were no patrons. That saloon was obviously bad for business. The next store was Buckman's, and Jack strolled in.

He took a quick look around the well-stocked emporium, noted it was also without customers, and then glanced at the storekeeper behind the counter. Jack touched his hat brim. "Howdy, mister. Guess I'll be giving you a little business."

"Sure could use some, friend." The man was small and wiry. His hair was black and slicked back. His thin face looked all the more so from the long waxed mustache.

Jack began gathering what he needed. After a couple of minutes, and with his arms full, he went up to the counter and laid everything down. As the storekeeper began weighing up the beans, flour, dried beef, and a few tins of fruit, he felt compelled to mention the obvious. "Business seems a little slow around here."

"Business is almost dead around here, mister." His expression showed disgust. "That saloon keeps any decent folks from coming anywhere near here. The worst sort of thieves and gunslingers frequent that snakepit. Can't blame people for avoiding this part of town altogether."

"Don't you have a marshal?"

"That's just it. The last marshal was killed in that place. The new one stays clear of this whole street."

Just then Jack noticed a couple men pass by. He got a pretty good look at them through the front window. They were coming from the direction of the saloon and were definitely gunmen. An uneasy feeling swept over him. There was a fair chance they were heading for the stable. He settled with the storekeeper quickly and stated, "Trouble only stays if you let it. There's other marshals." He picked up his supplies and added, "Good luck."

The storekeeper returned a grudging nod.

Jack went out the door and turned for the stable. There, close to the blacksmith's shop, were the two men he had just seen pass by the mercantile. Even from where he was, he could see the trouble brewing. The two gunhands had already spotted Fawn and were moving toward her, forcing her back against the hitching rail. Within a matter of moments, they were only a few feet from her and had her very frightened. Jack deliberately continued at a walk. He had experience with these sort of men. Running into a situation like that only starts the bullets flying sooner. He crossed the street and continued along a corral that ran parallel to the road all the way to the stable.

They were only interested in Fawn at the moment. When Jack got within about fifty paces of them, he was able to set the supplies down without them even seeing him. Just as he was doing so, Dan, apparently hearing the altercation, came through the stable doors. He didn't notice that Jack was a ways behind him. He just took one look at Fawn and the two gunhands and shouted, "You best leave her alone, boys!"

They were both young men, no more than twenty-five, and completely engrossed in taunting her. When they turned in response to Dan's challenge, it was easy to see the cockiness of youth in their faces. The one nearest to Dan spoke first. He was the taller, leaner, and older of the two. His words came with an air of confidence that comes when someone is convinced of his own invincibility. "Stay out of it, old man, if you want to keep on breathing." He glanced back at his partner, who now had a hold of Fawn's right arm, and gave a quick laugh. Then he turned back to Dan, adding, "Besides, we ain't anywhere near finished with this pretty little Injun gal."

Jack had been able to hear Dan and the gunman's exchange as he approached them. He walked up to Dan's right side and stopped. For a few seconds there was that time in which he and the two thugs simply stared at each other. Speaking casually, Jack broke the silence, "You can learn a lot from someone with experience. You two ought to listen to my friend Dakota, here."

"You're buttin' in where it ain't healthy, mister, and that old man wouldn't remember anything worth hearing!" The lean gunhand wasn't impressed by Jack's hardware or cool manner one bit.

Dan raised his eyebrows and looked the two men over. "At least I know the three rules of being a gunfighter."

The other gunman seemed to sense that things could get serious. He released Fawn's arm, and then positioned himself to the left side of his partner. The four men were only about a dozen feet apart. Fawn immediately went around to the blacksmith's shop for cover. The smithy had already found a safe place to watch. She joined him behind the water trough.

"What rules?" The taller man did the talking, but both men were running short on patience.

"Well, never holster an empty gun. Never face a man with the sun in your eyes. And most important: never, ever face a man that's a whole lot faster than you are."

"And what's your point, old-timer?" The lean man shook his head.

Dan gave his partner a little smile first and then began, "Now, I'm sure you two hombre's got bullets in those shooters. And that sun's way up in the sky. But when it comes to a gunfight, two out of three ain't that good." He gave Jack a little wink.

Briefly, the two gunman looked at each other with disbelief plainly showing on their faces. The shorter man then spoke. His voice was low and coarse. He spoke with a tone of arrogance as he stared at Jack. "I guess the old man thinks you're pretty fast with a gun, mister. Is that true?"

"Pretty fast," Jack stated as a matter of fact.

"Well, you're gonna die pretty fast, mister. And over a squaw?" He said it with smug grin.

Jack didn't like the last remark, and it showed. "We'll see." His voice was calm, but his eyes turned cold.

The lean man studied Jack's cool manner for a few more seconds, then glanced down at his hardware. "You got some fancy pistols there, mister. You got a name, too."

"McCall, Jack McCall."

"You the one they call, Diamondback McCall?" the shorter hombre asked with considerable surprise.

Jack answered with two nods, and then added, "So, now that you know who you're up against, how are you boys gonna play it—smart or stupid?"

The tall hombre was not only unimpressed, he was clearly hostile. "I ain't scared of some galoot that does tricks in some side show!"

"I see you're going for stupid." Jack seemed even less impressed.

"We don't take that from nobody!" The shorter man now shared his partner's anger.

"Fine. I'm not enjoying your company either." Jack paused for a few moments, waiting for them to make their move.

They didn't. Instead the tall one spurted out, "You picked the wrong men this time, McCall!"

Whether his tough words were to bolster his own courage or to try to throw a scare into Jack was hard to figure. Gunmen were always looking for an edge. In response, Jack merely shrugged and asked, "Then why are you just standing there? You gonna jaw, or you gonna draw?"

The tension of the next few moments grew. Jack could see what was going to happen; he'd seen it before. These two hombres were too young, too proud, and too sure of themselves to back down. They were going to draw, they just needed a little time to get their blood up. He could read their eyes and noted their twitchy right hands above their Colts. He probably knew when they were ready before they did. Still he waited. He let them make the first move. They went for their shooters and two guns fired at once! Jack's two .45s blasted lead into the two men's right shoulders before they managed to clear leather. They both reeled back and spun around to the right.

As Jack watched them each grab their bloodied upper arm and heard the moans as the pain took hold, he twirled his pistols back into their holsters. He stood there for a moment or two, not feeling good or bad about what just happened. It was simply necessary.

"I'll be taking those pistols, boys."

They were in no condition to resist or even complain.

Jack walked up to the two gunhands, pulled the Colts out of their holsters, and tossed them back to Dan. The two men had lost their cocky smirks. The confidence was no longer present in their eyes. They stood there looking at Jack, defenseless.

"You two don't know it, but I just did you a favor. No, I don't mean not killing you. I mean where I shot you." He shook his head slightly. "I got to tell you something, boys, you weren't that fast. But now, after what those bullets did to your shoulders, you can forget about guns." He gave a couple nods. "Time to think about some honest work. Time to get smart." He motioned toward downtown with his left hand. "Go on now. Get those tended to."

As they started back for town, Dan couldn't resist a parting comment. He called after them, "Someday you'll be able to tell your grandkids all about this. The day Diamondback McCall spared your miserable hides." He gave a little chuckle, but they headed into the business district without uttering a single word or even looking back. Jack watched them briefly and wondered if he would come to regret his leniency.

With the trouble clearly over, Fawn came running up to Jack and jumped up into his arms. He held her there tightly, with her feet dangling above the ground, and her arms wrapped around his neck. She pressed her cheek to his for a long moment and then whispered into his ear, "I wasn't scared, sweetheart. I knew you'd save me."

He took her by the waist and held her before him, "You really weren't afraid?" His expression showed some doubt.

She made a little pouting frown, "Well, maybe just a little."

He smiled and then pulled her close and kissed her gently. After letting her down to her feet, he gave a glance toward the saloon. He turned back to her and pursed his lips. "I think we better move on. Those two no-goods might have friends."

She nodded and started back to the smithy, who was back to work on her horse's loose shoe.

Dan had been standing off a bit to give the couple their few moments. As Jack headed back for the supplies he'd put on the ground, he saw that his partner was still grinning like a Cheshire cat. "So, did you find our little fracas interesting, partner?"

"Oh, it was lot's better than that. Heck, that was fun!"

"Good, but let's get out of here. I don't want any more fun today."

Dan just nodded and went back into the stable for the grain and cinch. Just like Jack, he'd set everything down to come to Fawn's aid. Within about ten minutes they both had the horses packed, and a new cinch strap was laced beneath Dan's saddle.

They walked their mounts over to the smithy, who had just finished the shoe repair. As Jack put his right hand into his pocket, the blacksmith held up both hands. "No sir, there's no charge. I'll be tellin' this story for a long time." The big man gave a little shake of the head. "Dangdest thing I ever saw. In fact I didn't see it. I didn't see those two pistols of yours 'til after you fired them."

"Well, much obliged." Jack reached out and shook the smithy's hand.

They then mounted up and continued north. There were six more days of tough riding. The mountains got higher and the passes steeper. While they made their way through valleys, canyons, and over mountainous crests, they had time to appreciate the lush landscape. Pine forests and red cliffs made for a vivid contrast. Streams and ponds, although smaller from the long summer, not only added to the scenery, but drew a variety of wildlife. From squirrels to elk, all sizes and manner of animals were in abundance. Jack had passed through these parts some years earlier; it was as he remembered, mighty pretty country.

The sun was dipping below the horizon as they entered the little settlement known as Williams. There was a purple glow in the west and a few dim lights filling the windows of the homes and the one business that made up this small town. This was their last stop for supplies before the Grand Canyon. Carson's Mercantile was the only business around for some miles. They also had a couple rooms to rent out back. After twelve days of sleeping under the stars, this would be a welcome change. After a night with real beds beneath them, they resupplied and headed north once again. It was twilight of the second day when they finally reached the great canyon. The dim light soon faded into darkness and with it, any chance of recognizing anything from the map. They laid out their bedrolls and tried to get some sleep, but all had a restless night of anticipation.

Chapter 6
Shadows and Light

The sun had not yet peaked over the far side of the canyon wall. An orange hue of pale light cast across that rugged silhouette of rock formations. There was a stillness in the air. Fawn and Dan continued to sleep while Jack quietly made his way to the edge of the great canyon. He held the ancient map up to his eyes, the dim light not being of much help. Jack loved a challenge and the quest for the golden hawk promised to be just that. He was anxious to get started. Soon the sun's first streaks of daylight would reveal the features of the rocky plateau above the canyon. There was still a shadowy darkness below him, but that too would soon be visible.

The leather map Jack held was nothing like what you would find at the General Land Office. It was done by ancient people, freehand and by memory. Nothing was to scale and several of the markings were a mystery to him. He had been able to figure out some of the symbols and they had led him to where he stood.

Now, as he gazed in both directions along the formations above the canyon, there was something unexpected. To his right, he saw a single beam of sunlight piercing the darkness far down into the canyon. He was looking east and that first slender shaft of light reflected off both walls in a zig-zag pattern. It was some distance to where that light found its way to the canyon floor. Jack leaned over the edge precariously, with fascination. The source of the light was at a point where the river made a slight bend. It had been flowing in a more southerly direction and then turned west. There was a V-shaped crack in the rocks on the far side of the bend and it went a ways down the canyon wall. The sun penetrated the gap in the wall, leaving the surrounding area in shadows. Some of that stream of light went straight across and above the canyon, illuminating with a widening swath the plateau on the other side. Jack's interest was in the beam that reflected back and forth on the canyon walls and down into the canyon.

He studied the relatively narrow area of the river made visible by the light. Nothing special could be seen. He noted flat-looking banks on both sides that probably would be below the waterline had it not been late summer, but that was all. Then, as the sun rose a little more and began to bring the entire canyon to light, he saw an image that raised the corners of his mouth. Above and to the right of the V-shaped crack in the canyon wall was a peculiarly shaped rock. It looked a lot like a flat mushroom, very much like the one on the

map. He took another look at the map. Was that lightening bolt supposed to be the beam of light he had just
seen pointing down into the canyon? That seemed
likely. Next was to find a way down.

Jack roused Dan and Fawn from their dreams with,
"Come on, you two. We've got things to do."

"What's the hurry, partner? We don't even know
where to start lookin'." Dan sat up while rubbing his
eyes. He didn't seem to share Jack's enthusiasm.

Fawn simply stood up and faced Jack with outstretched arms. After a brief hug, she stepped back and
took a long look around. "This is beautiful, where do
we start?"

He took her by the hand and led her to the very edge.
In many parts of the Grand Canyon the walls are terraced way back, creating the look of an enormous val-
ley. In the distance, where the river made the bend, it
was like that. But they were in an area of nearly vertical
canyon walls. She first looked straight down and Jack
continued to hold her hand firmly for reassurance. She
seemed to have no fear of heights and even leaned over
a little to see all she could. Jack saw the amazed expression on her face and knew, as she did, that the view
was beyond any words. When she finally looked up at
him and smiled, he motioned with his head to the right.
As she looked in the general direction of where the
canyon made the bend, he pointed with his left hand.
"See that rock formation that looks something like a
mushroom?"

She nodded.

He had the map in his right hand and gave it to her. As

she unrolled it and began studying it, he put his finger beneath the flat mushroom symbol. "Look familar?"

Her eyes moved from the map to the mushroom rock and back. "Is that really it?" There was surprise in the tone.

"Pretty sure. We've just got to head that way and try to find the path to the bottom."

"So what are we waiting for?"

"Dakota." Jack motioned toward his partner, who had laid down and gone back to sleep.

She saw him blissfully snoring away and grinned. "You get him up, and I'll get the horses."

Within minutes the horses were saddled, the bedrolls were tied down, and they were on their way. The sun was then high enough to see clearly. They rode along, keeping a comfortable distance from the canyon's edge for about ten minutes. Jack then held up his right hand, indicating a stop. He bounded down off Chilco and handed the reins to Dan. Fawn was just on the other side of Dan. Jack explained, "We're not going to find that trail into the canyon from here. We'll stop every so often, and I'll take a gander over the side."

He went to the edge, laid on his stomach, and pulled himself as far as safely possible over the abyss. He stared down and in each direction. No luck—just the rugged canyon wall and river below. He rejoined the others and tried again, unsuccessfully, a few hundred feet farther along. And so it went for three more tries. Then after a quarter mile or so, and as he once again peered down, he saw a narrow and steep ledge. It was all the way at the bottom and looked pretty close to where the beam of light had pointed. From there it angled up and to the right, but disappeared from view as the canyon wall veered slightly right. Whether it was the path that the Indians used or just a natural occurence that didn't go the entire way up was the question. They rode ahead again and Jack made another survey. There it was again, and it was now considerably higher. He started getting a little excited.

The terrain had been mostly flat on their side of the canyon since they started that morning. More interesting formations were to be seen on the other side. The bend in the canyon lay just ahead. As they rode, all three found themselves gazing across the expanse of the canyon. They seemed captivated by the *V*-shaped crack in the canyon wall and that odd mushroomlike rock. Jack thought to himself that no one tires of a treasure hunt. His attention was then drawn to two large, flat rocks at the very edge. He then noticed that there was a narrow depression sloping down into the canyon that went between the rocks. Without hesitation, he jumped down and went for a look. The two red rocks were roughly waist-high and were almost square. The weathered six-foot-wide formations stood prominent along the otherwise level section of plateau. Jack thought they looked like a grand entrance and that was just what they were. He passed between them and followed the path a little ways down as it turned to the left and then headed downward. There he stood, looking down the narrow ledge that would take them all the way to the bottom. When Jack returned, he didn't have to explain. He just had a big smile. They could see from his expression that he'd found the entrance.

It took a little time to unpack and tend to the horses. While Jack gathered what he needed for the river, Dan tied their reins to a heavy rock and then gave all three ponies enough grain and water to hold them until they returned. Fawn busied herself with breakfast. Since they were anxious to get started, it consisted only of some strips of dried beef and canned peaches. They finished the meager meal, picked up the few things needed, and started down.

Jack carried two long ropes around his neck, his saddlebag over his left shoulder, and the goat-stomach water bag in his right hand. The saddlebag contained the map, a little food, and some dry clothes. Dan had the canteens and a rifle. It was a long way to the bottom and back so they brought no more than what they figured to be necessary.

At first there was some shoulder room because the canyon wall had a gentle slope. Farther down it grew tight as they got to the section of vertical wall. Jack led the way down the steep, narrow, and occasionally broken path. Fawn followed behind him so he could reach back and take her hand when required.

There were a number of broken spots along the path where a small section of the ledge had disappeared. Most were small enough to simply step across. There were a couple others that were far more challenging. With a gap of several feet in which there was nothing but daylight beneath them, it took a different approach. Jack would first jump across and then await Fawn and Dan in turn with an outstretched hand. He was able to then grab their hands easily and pull them toward him. Jack didn't find it too surprising that some of the path had crumbled during the past few centuries, but he was glad it wasn't in any worse condition.

The descent went without any real drama. Fawn took the altitude and the broken pathway calmly. From the tense expression on his face, Dan did not enjoy the trip down, but he said nothing. He did, however, seem much happier once they reached the bottom.

Chapter 7
Dark Passage

The river narrowed where they stood. Jack knew that meant it was deeper there. The current also seemed to run a little slower here than upstream, although for what Jack had to do, he wished it was flowing slower still. There was a pretty long stretch of flat, rocky bank where the water funneled down through the narrow section. Up and downstream of the banks, the river flowed all the way against the canyon walls.

While Dan and Fawn seemed awed by the size, scope, and sheer beauty of the canyon, Jack was the very picture of concentration. He set everything but the map down and carefully viewed every detail before him, section by section. There were still symbols on the map with unknown meaning. So far, that map had done a good job of leading the way. He knew it would save a lot of time if it could narrow the search once more.

Jack took another hard look at those last two symbols. One looked like an *L* laying on its side with a dot above it. To the left of that was what resembled a horizontal hourglass. These two symbols made no sense to Jack, and he saw nothing even vaguely similar before him. They were placed just below and to the left of the mushroom rock and *V*, so he figured they must be nearby. It finally occurred to him that it might be his perspective at the river's edge that was throwing him. Perhaps he was just too close. He turned back for the path and climbed up a ways before he stopped and gave the area a wider scan.

As he looked to the right, his eyes got a little wide. He put his hands on his hips and gave a couple shakes of the head. *Could that be it?,* he wondered. *Is that* L *simply the route of the river?* He then took another glance below, where the river became narrow. *And that's the hourglass,* he mused. It was, indeed, a lot like the symbol on the map.

Since that conclusion made more sense to him than anything else, he brought the map back to Dan and Fawn to see if they agreed. They did. And at first their expression's lit up with excitement. But then, Fawn's face changed to concern. She looked over at river with its muddy brown color and steady current and then back to Jack. "You know, I've been as anxious as you to get here and find that golden idol, but somehow, I thought the river would be lower. I thought you'd be able to see the cave and . . . well, at least be able to breathe down there."

"Yeah, partner, how you gonna find that cave, let alone go inside it all that way on one gulp of air?" Dan had queried with a doubtful look on his face.

Jack smiled, "I've got a plan. You've always got to have a plan."

"You mind sharin' it with us?" Dan asked the question that was surely on Fawn's mind as well.

"Well, you two are half of it. While I'm in the water, you'll be hanging on to the lifeline." He pointed over to the two long ropes. "The rest is up to me and that water bag." It was obvious that they didn't understand, so he added, "You'll see, it's simple."

He went over to the two ropes and tied them together. He then tied one end around his waist. "The first thing is to get all of us on the other side. The chief said that cave was on the far side. So you two hang on to the end of this rope. I'll be the first one to get wet."

After removing his boots, holster, and hat, he laid them with the saddlebag and water bag. He then went upstream as far as the bank went, about ten paces. The bank was not so wide at that point, so he didn't have a lot of running room. He sprinted those first ten steps and then dove into the water. Of course he knew the current would take him downstream. There was only about forty feet of bank on the other side, then it went back to a sheer vertical canyon wall. But between the running start and his strength as a swimmer, he made it to the other side with several feet to spare. From that point, he managed to scramble out of the water and up onto the bank. With the first step completed, he stood up and headed back upstream, across from Dan and Fawn.

He motioned for them to move toward the river. When they were near the edge, he called to Dan, "Take up the slack and then tie it just under her arms."

Dan nodded and knew just what came next. As Fawn entered the river, they kept the rope high and tight. She faced downstream and let the current take her legs out before her. Slowly Jack pulled her toward his side, while Dan maintained the tension to keep her head above the water.

With that completed, it was Dan's turn. "How you figure on gettin' me over there, Jack? I don't swim so good."

"Tie the end of that rope up under your arms, Dakota, just like you did on Fawn."

He did, but it was easy to see, even from across the river, that he didn't like it.

Jack then motioned toward the gear he'd left on the bank. "See that water bag?"

He gave a nod.

"Take the plug out of the spout and then blow some air in it."

Dan suddenly knew what the bag was really for and all worry seemed to disappear from his face. He did as Jack directed, replaced the plug and then gave him a couple nods.

"Good. Now slide that thing under your shirt and hang on to it while I pull you over."

Dan sat down on the edge for just a moment and then worked his way down into the water. Immediately the current took him racing downstream. The air-filled bag did its job of keeping him afloat, but he did a fair amount of bobbing and turning as Jack fought to reel him in. In fact, it wasn't just Jack doing the pulling. He was quite grateful for Fawn's efforts on the rope. They slowly pulled Dan back and over to the bank. Jack then reached down with his right hand, grabbed Dan's wrist, and lifted him up onto the bank. Jack immediately untied the rope from Dan's chest while leaving the other end still tied around his own waist.

"So what happens next?" Fawn still had some concern in her voice.

"Time to find that cave. While I'm poking around down there, you two will have to hold me back. Otherwise I'm going for a long ride."

They both gave a reluctant nod and followed him back upstream, where the bank began.

"That map seems to show the cave is somewhere along this narrow part of the canyon. That figures because this is the hardest rock I've seen along here. The rest of this red sandstone is too soft, it would've collapsed from the current." He tried to show a reassuring smile. "Now we've got less than fifty feet to explore. Easy, right?"

Dan and Fawn looked at each other briefly and the shrugged their shoulders.

"Well, let's get started." He went to the water's edge with them just behind. "Give me about fifteen foot of slack."

They did.

"Now, don't let me pull you two in here too. I don't think the current's that strong, but if you have to, let me go. I'll figure a way out."

They gave each other one more look and braced themselves. Jack then dived, head first, into the muddy brown water. Dan and Fawn felt the slack run out, and the pressure of the current and the effect of Jack's efforts to swim downward against the rope. It was manageable. Jack's job was tougher. It wasn't only that he could see very little, it was also extremely difficult to stay down. Between the current and the angle of the rope, he was being pulled back up. It took a lot of hard swimming to overcome that and he used up his oxygen quickly. Still, he was able to find the bottom and probe with his hands against the solid rock wall. It wasn't going to be easy or fast, but it was working.

He came up for air, put his arms up onto the bank, and breathed heavily for a couple minutes. Fawn and Dan then moved a couple steps downstream so he would be able to explore the next section, and he was soon at it again. Dive and rest, section by section, on and on. After almost a half hour, with fatigue and frustration setting in, he came back up smiling. Once he got his breath back, he managed, "Think I found it."

He pulled himself up onto the bank, lay down on his back and closed his eyes. As he rested, Fawn sat beside him and brushed his wet hair back off his forehead with her hand. He opened his eyes and gazed fondly at her. "How's my girl doing?"

"I'm fine, but how about you? And how are you supposed to breathe inside that cave?"

He turned to Dan, who was standing upstream a little and doing what he usually did when Jack and Fawn were together—looking the other way. "Could you bring me that water bag behind you, Dakota?"

He brought it over. "I gotta admit I've been wonderin' the same dang thing. Ain't that a long time to hold your breath?"

"Too long. That's why I'm taking this along with me." He held the water bag before him. "I figure there's enough air in here to get me through."

"Will that work?" Fawn didn't seem to share his optimism.

"Well, I'm counting on it. Anyway, I'm sure gonna find out in a hurry if it doesn't."

Once again Dan and Fawn simply looked at each other with the usual blank stares.

Jack busied himself with the water bag. About twelve feet back from where the rope was tied around his wrist, he started lacing the rope around the water bag. He interwove it so the bag was virtually encased in a rope net. Satisfied that the bag couldn't slip out, he got ready to give it a try.

Jack directed them on where to stand and how much slack he needed. He judged where to enter so he wouldn't be dragged beyond the cave entrance by the current. Finally he looked back and gave last instructions. "Just hold it steady while I work my way in. When you feel two tugs on the rope, that means I'm in. So then give some more slack so I can pull the bag down. From there, just let the rope slip as I go in." He started to dive in, but then glanced back again, realizing he'd left out one detail. "If you feel the rope tugging hard and fast, pull me in fast. That means I'm in trouble."

They gave a couple nods, and Jack dove in. Again, he had to work against the rope and current and that tended to use up his oxygen faster. His aim was pretty good, though, and it wasn't long before he found the cave and was able get his hands inside the top of the entrance to pull himself inside. The natural buoyancy of his body caused him to raise upward and settle against the roof of the cave. He worked his way far enough into the blackish passage to turn sideways. Then he gave two tugs on the rope. It was a little harder to pull the air-filled bag down than he would have guessed. If he pulled too fast it started to dislodge him, causing him to slide back out, instead of bringing the bag down. It had to be done slowly and smoothly. Meanwhile, Jack was getting a little desperate for air.

Even though he was near the cave entrance and some of the sun's rays penetrated that far into the murky water, visibility was almost nil. He continued to gradually pull the bag toward him, while fighting to control the normal instinct of panic. He couldn't tell how close it was until he finally felt the end-knot of the lacing around the bag. His source of air was at hand, now came the tricky part: how to fill his lungs without losing too much air from the spout. Jack was already starting to get light-headed, but he tried to think logically. He quickly pulled the bag to his chest with the spout to his mouth. Then he turned so he was facing down. He pinched off the leather neck of the bag with his right hand and removed the wooden plug with his left. While palming the plug, he slid the spout into his mouth. Then he used his thumb and forefinger to hold his nose and released the pinch on the bag of air. He exhaled through his nose and breathed in through his mouth. It worked well enough, but he knew his air supply was limited. After three breaths, he returned the plug and started moving farther into the cave.

Jack reasoned that he would be able to go faster if he had the full use of his hands. He left the bag behind, knowing he could pull it to him when needed.

Negotiating an underwater passage in total darkness

has its share of challenges and hazards. But Jack couldn't dwell on that; he had to find the end of that cave before he ran out of air. He stayed up by the jagged roof so he could use the jutting rocks to pull himself along. Then he reached out from time to time with both hands and touched the walls of the narrow passage to stay centered. It worked pretty well, though it had its risks. The last thing he wanted to do was strike his head against one of the protruding rocks. So he did what he always did in a tight situation, measured the odds and got on with it, anyway.

After a minute or so, he felt the roof suddenly go up. At first he wondered if he was near the end of the passage, remembering that the chief said it did just that. Then he abruptly found out how wrong he was as he hit headlong into a mound of loose rocks. It was a glancing blow that caused him to tumble upward. Momentarily, confusion hung over him as he tried to regain his sense of direction and determine just what he had hit. As he flailed his hands around what felt like a pile of debris, it suddenly made sense. It was a cave-in. Jack had been in mines and had seen cave-ins. Sometimes they completely sealed the passage, but just as often there could be an opening at the very top.

He scrambled up to the top of the mound while feeling a renewed urgency for air. In the center, where the roof met the mound, he felt a small opening. He put his hands in as far as possible—it seemed to go all the way through. Probing its oblong diameter, he figured that he could pass through with a little room to spare. Jack had to make a decision and he had to make it fast. Of course, being cautious was not in Jack's nature. Nor was quitting. He simply calculated that the odds weren't that bad. For all he knew, that cave-in could have happened a century ago. He figured the chances of the roof coming down on him right then was remote. He wasn't going to be in there that long. As he reached up to the roof to plant his hands on a couple of protruding stones, he began sliding his feet into the claustrophobic hole. It wasn't until he had gotten all the way to the widest point of his chest that he realized the flaw in his thinking. At that point it was tight. In fact, he had to keep his arms above his head to squeeze by. He started to feel small stones coming loose all around his torso and neck while he squirmed by those last few inches. He now had to deal with a severe need of air and the sudden realization that he just might be setting a cave-in in motion by disturbing things.

He was just about through. With a turn of the head and a little help from his feet, he slid the rest of the way through. His hands were the last things to pass by that little passage and he still felt some tiny stones that he had brushed against falling, but that was it, no cave-in. Now, with his lungs feeling like they could burst and every second without air pure torture, he reeled in the bag. He did it smoothly, so he wouldn't confuse those above tending the rope.

It was getting more difficult for him to think with clear reason. Even a man like Jack McCall would lose some powers of judgment with a lack of oxygen. He pulled the spout to his mouth and used his earlier method for three more small breaths. That just about depleted the air in the bag.

The breaths revived his senses, and he pushed off again. He moved quickly for what he hoped would soon be the end of the passage and his quest. There were some lingering doubts traveling with him. He didn't have any way of knowing how far the cave went before it was supposed to go up. He also had second thoughts about his decision to continue past the cave-in. He wondered if the lack of oxygen influenced that decision. Those sorts of thoughts were not helpful, so he brushed them aside.

He moved on through the eerie black passage until there was finally a subtle change. Total darkness gave way to a faint glow above his head. It was an almost round shape of pale yellow light. Jack instantly started swimming upward for the light, which seemed to get larger as it became closer. Suddenly, and none too soon, his head abruptly emerged from the water. Air was his immediate concern. If it was good air or bad, it didn't matter; he was out of time and options. He filled his lungs and didn't mind that it was stale and musty. Then, while still breathing hard and slowly moving his hands and feet to tread water, he turned to look around the small cavity he found himself in. It was like a small dome, although much higher than it was wide. He could easily touch each side with his hands. Visibility was only fair, with a single ribbon of light that penetrated the cavity from the very top. A tiny crack above let that thin strand of sunlight inside. It pointed almost straight down to the water.

In spite of the dim light, he could see the object he had come for. About five feet above him was what looked a little like an altar. Carved into the far wall was a two-foot square recess. Displayed prominently on this obviously man-made shelf was a statue. It looked every bit like the hawk the chief had described and was over a foot tall. But if it was gold, it didn't look the part. It was the same drab brownish color as the rock it rested on. Either way Jack was taking it with him. He had come too far to go back empty-handed.

With his panting subsiding, he started preparing. First he pulled the air bag up to him—he would need it going back. Then he began working his way up the narrow shaft. There were plenty of footholds with the jagged rock walls. So he simply spread his feet apart and pushed outward against both walls. He steadied himself with his hands and slowly edged his way up. It wasn't long before he was nearly eye-level with the bird. At that point, he put his weight on his left hand to remain steady while he reached for his prize. It was surprisingly heavy. He brought it to his chest and rubbed the head on his wet shirt. Then he held it up to the strand of light. He smiled as he remembered the saying, nothing glitters like gold.

As he began using his belt to secure the idol to the front of his waist for the return trip, he saw something else. It was the same color as the shelf it rested on, so Jack had nearly missed it. Brown dust had settled on it as it had on the hawk. He reached out and picked up what looked very much like the map that had led him there. In the dim light, it was hopeless to try and read it. Instead he pulled the the bag up to where he was. He then took out the plug, rolled the scroll up tight, and slid it into the bag. Not wanting to risk getting the ancient leather scroll wet, he went ahead and refilled the bag with air from his mouth before returning the plug. He then eased himself back into the water. It was time to head back. Jack held on to a rock and began taking deep breaths in anticipation of the venture. He spun forward, kicked his feet straight up, and swam down to where the cave turned back. He found it easier since the statue's weight helped pull him down. The extra weight made him feel almost neutral as he didn't tend to float up as much as before. Things were going well. Soon he was back to the cave-in.

Jack decided to go ahead and take a breath or two, even though he still felt alright. He wanted to make sure his mind stayed alert and figured the bag would pass by more easily if partly deflated. After going through the same routine as earlier, he located the small opening and pushed the air bag and excess rope through. Now was his turn. Not wanting to be separated from the air supply or his lifeline, he thought headfirst was the smart play. He also remembered that opening was none too big the last time through and thought the idol might just hang him up. After working it out of his belt, he had no choice but to hold on to it until he got by the tight part.

He went in facedown with his arms stretched out ahead to make his shoulders as small as possible. Once he got his head through, he began using his upper arms and elbows to force his shoulders by. A scattering of tiny pebbles began showering down around his neck and on his back. He squirmed and pushed until his shoulders and chest were free. At the same time, more debris started falling and it wasn't just small stones anymore. It had also filled in the opening around him and it would take some strength and leverage to get free.

Jack knew he had to get out fast and he needed both hands. His first instinct was to simply drop the statue and think only of escape. But Jack couldn't abide failure. He risked the extra second or two it took to slide it down into his shirt. Then he pushed off as hard as he could with both hands while the roof rained down a hail of rocks. Just at the point where only his lower legs needed to come through, the roof above his legs gave way. Jack felt the weight and pain as it hit. What was the roof just a moment before began sliding down and around Jack's waist. He was stuck and it was only going to get worse. There was only one hope, and he knew it. With his customary speed, he reeled in the slack in the rope and gave it hard and rapid tugs. Immediately, he felt the rope begin to pull and pull hard on his waist. At the same time, he pushed off with his hands for all he was worth and tried to move his legs to loosen the cave-in's grip on him.

He could feel his legs inching ahead and the shifting rubble coming in behind his feet at the same time. Jack was working hard and using up what little air was left in his lungs. He was in trouble. Although the combined force on the rope and his own strength was dragging him out, he was running out of time. He gave one more violent push while pulling his legs forward. Suddenly, they broke loose from the rocks and the roof gave way even more. Jack felt a cascade of debris pelting him as he was being quickly towed out of the dark and crumbling passage. Moments later, he was pulled up onto the river's bank.

He lay there on his back and gasped for air. It took a while for his wind, mind, and vision to return. He looked up at the worried expressions on Dan and Fawn and forced a smile. "See, that wasn't so bad."

Chapter 8
The Island

The sun had already settled behind the mountains when they rode into the Papago village. A purple sky was giving way to gray clouds and twilight brought a brief richness of color across the desert. The unrelenting summer heat had made for a tough twelve days in the saddle. They intended to stay the night and the next day there at the village and then head back to Spirit Feather the following nightfall.

They spent the night, which had become usual for them, sleeping under the stars. Shortly after daybreak, they wandered down to the river to wash up. Jack carried his saddlebags along over his shoulder. They contained his shaving gear and also the golden hawk. He wasn't about to leave that unattended. By the time they had finished their morning clean-up routine, the cooking fires were well under way in the village, and those smells drew them back to the area where the tribe did business. They soon found their favorite cook, a round and cheerful woman who was more than happy to take their order. After finishing a typical Papago breakfast of beans, tortillas, and corn, they headed for the mission. They planned to hole up inside the mission for the day. It was both safer and far cooler to wait for dark. In the meantime, the mission's thick walls would give them some relief from the heat.

Fawn's classroom was within the mission itself. It was originally used as a storage room by the Jesuit priests. Since the Jesuit's abandonment of Mission San Xavier, the Papago tribe not only held services in the chapel, they also made good use of its many rooms. Her classroom was adjacent to a large and beautiful patio behind the mission. The center piece was a large fountain with walkways and gardens surrounding it. The classroom had four windows facing the patio, which let in light and allowed a pleasant view of the grounds.

Fawn's students were always small in number and tended to be young. The older children were needed to help out in the fields and in the day-to-day effort of surviving in a harsh land. With the summer heat and the daily necessity of hauling water, even the smaller children were needed. So Jack and friends utilized the unattended room for the day.

There were two, eight-foot-long, dark oak tables, one behind the other, in front of the teacher's small oak desk. Four smallish chairs were pushed under each table, facing the desk. Jack laid his saddlebags down on the back table. Soon, he and Dakota ended up using the table nearest to the desk for a little diversion. They sat there, whiling away the time, with a game of poker.

Jack couldn't help but notice Fawn's activity with the bookshelves that covered most of the wall behind the desk. At first he thought she was simply doing a little housekeeping, but it soon became apparent that she was looking for something. She slowly went along, shelf by shelf, pulling the occasional book out briefly for a closer look. Finally, she seemed to find what she was searching for. She then went around the desk and put one large, but rather thin book, *Mexico*, on the table by Jack. Immediately, she was back at it again, going through her little library. Pretty soon, she held what looked like a very old, yellow, handwritten journal. As she laid it beside the other book, Jack noticed that it was written in Spanish. *Historias de Soldados* was written atop the front cover. The name, Padre Luis Flores, was signed at the lower right corner.

Fawn walked around to the back table and opened up the left saddlebag. She carefully pulled out the scroll that Jack had found within the cave and then rejoined the two men at cards. The game had momentarily paused while Jack and Dan silently watched and wondered what she was up to.

She unrolled the fragile brown leather script. Midway along what was clearly a coastline on the ancient map, she pointed to a particular spot and turned to Jack. "Ever since you first came out of that cave and showed me this, I've been thinking about this island." It did, indeed, appear to be a tiny island close to a shoreline.

"What's so special about the island?" Jack asked as he leaned over and studied it a little closer.

"It shouldn't be there."

"I don't follow you."

She reached for the book on Mexico, placed it before him and opened it to the third page. It was a complete map of the Mexican mainland. She ran her finger along the eastern coast, from just above the Yucatan Peninsula, up to the Rio Grande. Jack then took the ancient scroll and moved it beside the book's map. It was only a partial map. The handwritten script included just a shoreline, the sea, and some islands. It did not require long comparison. In fact, it was obvious that the old map was of the same coastline.

Once again Fawn placed a finger beneath the small island just offshore on the ancient map. Then she moved her finger over to the map in the Mexican book. "This is where that island should be, just offshore of Rio Antigua, about fifteen miles north of Vera Cruz." She looked over to Jack and smiled, "But it's not there."

"Maybe it's just a mistake."

"I don't think so." She reached for the old journal, placed it beside the old map, and briefly pointed to the title. "When I first came here to make this a classroom, I found this at the bottom of a pile of papers over there in the corner." She motioned behind her with a turn of the head. "One long, cold night, when I couldn't sleep, I decided to brush up on my Spanish. I started reading this journal. *Soldiers' Tales* is the title, and that's what's in this book. When the Spanish army used to pass through this area, this mission was always a place where they would stop. And this is the journal of one of the padres in residence at the time. He started writing down the adventures and tales that were told to him by the soldiers. It became, apparently, a hobby with him. In the beginning of the book he tells of how he would greet the troops and ask them if they knew any stories worth telling. So he heard a lot of accounts of battles and discoveries, and they're here in his journal. There were also some tales of legends past. That's where this island comes in."

Jack and Dan exchanged shrugged shoulders as Fawn flipped through about half of the journal's pages. She held the book open with her left hand and turned to Jack and Dan. "I didn't take much notice of this story at the time. It sounded a lot like an Aztec parable to me, not a true story. But when I saw that old map, I remembered this legend and wondered . . ."

"Wondered what?" Jack laid down his cards as he started getting curious.

"I wondered if we could find it."

He lowered his eyebrows, showing a perplexed expression. "The island that's not there?" He looked to Dan, who seemed equally puzzled.

She gave a wide smile and nodded her head. "Okay, let me tell you the story and you'll see what I mean." She settled into a chair, laid the journal in her lap, and perused it for a few moments. After refreshing her memory of some of the details, she began. It wasn't necessary for her to read the whole account, she just wanted them to get the general idea. "Well, the story is called 'La Isla De Oro Illuminata'—'The Island Of Golden Light.' It tells of an island directly offshore of a river and just beyond the horizon, and how the high priest of Zempoala, which is close to Vera Cruz, ordered a great temple built on the island. It was to honor the sun god and had a great golden sun placed at the very top of a pyramid. It seems that there was a burst of light reflected off the golden sun at twilight, which was where it got its name. It was said to be such a brilliant glow that it looked like fire coming out of the sea. But then the high priest embraced a different god, Quetzalcoatl, the plumed serpent. This so enraged the sun god, that he wreaked destruction on the city and the island disappeared into the sea." Having finished with the gist of the story, she looked to Jack and Dan for their reaction. She noted that they still seemed a little puzzled. She then smiled and prompted with, "Well?"

Jack glanced to Dan, who was wearing a doubtful expression, turned back to Fawn and nodded. "Well, it's intriguing, that's for sure. But how can we know if this really happened? I mean it might be just what you first thought. A story warning against worshipping false gods."

"Sure, it might be, but I don't think so. I think it was an earthquake or some sort of volcanic action that destroyed the city and caused the island to sink. The people simply attached 'the wrath of god' to a natural occurrence. You know, there are volcanoes in the area." She said it as a matter of fact, like she was teaching a class.

Jack gave the two maps another long study. Then he leaned back in his chair and considered all Fawn's evidence. He wanted to believe it—he loved a challenge—but it seemed kind of thin.

Fawn, noticeably anxious, interrupted his thoughts. "So, what do you think?"

"Well, what do you figure the odds?"

She twisted her mouth a little, knowing they weren't that good. "Maybe fifty-fifty." Even that was probably optimistic.

As Jack listened to her answer and gazed into her dark and persuasive eyes, he realized that the odds really didn't matter. She desperately wanted to go on this venture, he sensed with certainty. Jack surely loved her, but he also understood the lure of adventure and prized her independent spirit. She was an exceptional woman, and he wasn't about to disappoint her. He looked fondly to Fawn and gave one firm nod. "Okay, I guess we're going to Vera Cruz." He turned to his partner. "What about you, Dakota?"

"Heck fire, if you're headin' south of the border, I'm goin' too." His eyes narrowed some. "You plan on goin' after that sun made out of gold?"

"We're not going that far just for the tamales."

Dan's expression and voice still hinted of doubt. "Well, just how you plan on findin' it, let alone bringin' it up? That's a whole lot of water out there."

Jack lowered his eyebrows and seemed, momentarily, lost in thought. As Fawn and Dan looked and waited for his answer, he finally smiled awkwardly and shrugged. "I don't know, but that's part of the challenge, figuring it out."

"Okay, partner, you mosey down there for the challenge. I'll tag along for the tamales."

Chapter 9
Coming Home

Once they were convinced of the possibility of finding the sunken island and committed to the venture, one thing became evident. It made little sense for all three to make the long ride back to Spirit Feather, especially since the Southern Pacific was in the other direction. Jack, however, had to make the trip. He was the one that told the chief that he would bring back the golden hawk, and he would fulfill that promise. It was quickly decided that Dan and Fawn would wait for his return at the mission. They could use the rest before facing another long journey.

So Jack made the trek to the hidden city alone—an uneventful ride across the desert under a warm night sky. With about an hour before first light, he entered the boxed canyon, rolled the stone door open, and led Chilco to the stable within the upper cavern. After tending to his mount and retrieving the idol from the saddlebag, he went to the doorway leading to the main cavern and started down the long wooden ladders.

In the upside-down world of the hidden city, it was nearly the end of their day and many were already in their beds. When Jack reached the platform where he would change to the lower ladder, the few people still in the plaza spotted him. By the time he stepped off the second ladder and onto the plaza floor, the word of his arrival had begun to spread. He held the idol before him and walked toward the center of the courtyard, which was near the fountain. Suddenly there was a throng of voices as people approached him from all directions. It seemed that everyone in the village poured into the plaza at once and surrounded him. A joyous swell of smiling faces greeted him and took him by surprise.

It wasn't until that moment that Jack knew how much the idol meant to these people. He realized what it must have represented to them. This had been a missing part of their past. A symbol of who they were, where they had come from, and what they believed.

Soon the crowd began to separate, making way for the chief, his son Tenkee, and Chota, who was just a few steps behind. They made their way through the gathered masses and then, as they stopped just before him, Jack presented the idol to the chief with outstretched arms. For several seconds Tecanay simply held it close to his eyes, almost as if he were in a trance. Finally, he held it high in his right hand and turned, full circle, so all could see. There was a spontaneous response with cheering voices and raised hands throughout the crowd. After a half minute or so, with the excitement and volume diminished, Tecanay passed the golden hawk to his son and turned back to Jack. He put both hands on Jack's shoulders, looked him straight in the eyes, and gave him one quick nod. Jack returned the nod, realizing that the chief was right. In moments like this, words were unnecessary.

In less than an hour, Jack was in his usual quarters. The din of voices were by then muted and he, like the rest of the village, was heading for bed.

He had given Chota the briefest account of what was involved in retrieving the idol. It was Jack's nature to understate things, especially when speaking of himself. It was a similar case with the pending venture to Mexico. He saw no purpose in mentioning a quest for sunken treasure. Jack doubted that Chota, let alone the others of the village, would understand his need for travel and adventure. They were a people content to live their lives within the confines of the cavern city. So he told Chota that he simply had some matters to attend to and asked him to pass that along to the chief.

For all but the first hour or so, Jack had slept soundly. There had been the sound of hammering on rock, which must have kept others awake as well. Chota had joined him for breakfast, as usual, but few words were spoken. It always seemed to Jack that Chota could sense when he was about do something risky, even if he had told him otherwise. He gave Jack a worried expression when they exchanged farewells.

It was morning in the village but early evening in the outside world. As Jack walked along the plaza on his way to the first ladder, he saw the result of the hammering that had kept him awake. Near the top of ceremonial Kiva was a carved recess, very much like the one within the cave where he had first found the idol. Standing prominently in the recessed altar was the golden hawk. It seemed to Jack that it was home, where it belonged. As he continued for the ladder, it occurred to him that the chief had been far from certain of its return. The fact that they had not carved it's new home earlier, suggested just that.

A couple hours later, Jack was back aboard Chilco. It was warm like the previous night. Only the glow of a half-moon lit his way as he headed back to the mission. The long hours were passed with occasional thoughts of the looming adventure and by simply taking in the desert landscape by moonlight. Dark shapes and long shadows surrounded him—an eerie contrast of black and gray. It was a night of stillness and without a hint of wind. Just the sounds of his horse's hooves and sometimes an owl or a coyote in the distance. In the quiet, there was time for thinking. The seeds of a plan for the lost island were in his mind. Jack always had a plan.

Chapter 10
Galveston Bay

J ack had ridden all night to get back to the mission and arrived mid-morning. He could see excitement in Fawn's and Dan's eyes. It was obvious that they were anxious to begin their long trip to Vera Cruz.

Just how they would find the island and retrieve the golden sun once there was another matter. Jack had a basic plan, some rough ideas, but he needed time to think them through and chose not to mention them yet. When it came to the route, there weren't many choices. Going overland was out of the question. The desert and subsequent jungle were major obstacles. That left a sea voyage. It was decided to make their way down to Galveston Bay by rail and then travel south by ship from there.

All three were used to traveling light. To that end, Jack and Dan decided to leave their rifles and long ropes behind. It was also inappropriate to carry heavy weapons among city folk. Besides, Jack figured on having what ropes and equipment for the diving made in Mexico. So they had each rolled a change of clothes and a few grooming items within their bedrolls, securing each one with three short lengths of rope. Fawn also included a map of eastern Mexico. She thought it would be foolish to go into unknown country without a map. It took but a moment to tear the map page from the book on Mexico and mark the spot where the island was supposed to be with an *X*. Below the *X* she wrote, optimistically, *La Isla De Oro Illuminata.*

Dan remembered that the Southern Pacific had a train departing for El Paso, San Antonio, and finally Houston around nine in the evening. That gave them time to head into Tucson in the afternoon, stable their horses, and still make the train.

It was fortunate that Jack had saved most of the money he had earned from the time he spent in the show. Actually, it had been easy. Going endlessly from town to town left little time to spend it. He had over two hundred dollars in his pocket. More than enough for their expedition south.

Jack didn't mind risking money on a long shot and the venture they were beginning was certainly that. Taking risks and bucking the odds was simply a part of his life. In fact, it was the challenge far more than the gold that fascinated him. Figuring out just how he could beat the odds would be on his mind along the way.

The eastbound train rolled out of Tucson a little past 9 P.M. Dan watched the station disappear as he gazed out of the window. Meanwhile, Jack tipped his Stetson down over his eyes to try and catch some sleep. Fawn was between the two men and knew her man had to be tired. He hadn't closed his eyes since leaving the Anasazi village.

There were only about a dozen fellow passengers sharing the coach that evening, and the car's rocking motion soon had them all asleep. The train continued eastward, making the occasional whistle stop, on into the night. Sunlight piercing the car's windows stirred them from their slumber the following morning. A few hours later, they had seen El Paso come and go.

Whether watching the parched countryside pass by from the dining car or sitting back in their coach, the time went by slowly. The landscape was bleak and the temperature stifling. Day turned to night, and then a little after midnight San Antonio was behind them. Jack noticed a change in the climate as the tracks led them nearer the Gulf Coast. The dry desert air was being replaced by a thick, sultry atmosphere. A full moon that night allowed a murky view of the landscape as it passed by the car's window. Subtropical vegetation made for a vivid contrast to the stark, arid country they had just come through.

The sun had appeared only about an hour before the weary travelers stepped down from the train at Houston Station. Minutes later they were on board a hired carriage that awaited passengers just outside the station. The driver soon delivered them to a freight office on Buffalo Bayou, Port of Houston.

There were two ways to travel down the narrow passage to Galveston Bay, a stream that was neither wide nor deep enough for ocean-going ships. Barges and small steamships routinely carried cargo down the inlet to the Port of Galveston. The steamships were faster;

Jack booked a one way trip on the next run. Although the small white, single-stack craft was loaded with cotton bales from bow to stern, there was room for three passengers up in the pilot house. They shared a commanding view with a burly seaman at the wheel. As the stern-wheeled vessel eased down the brush-and-tree-lined passage, Jack was able to learn what he needed from the talkative helmsman. All ships in the Port of Galveston were registered with the port authorities. The ship's name, berth, previous port, and destination would be on record there. It was just a matter of walking down to the harbormaster's office and finding a vessel going on to Vera Cruz.

It was just past noon by the time the steamship was moored. Once it was tied off to one of the many slips attached to a wharf that ran along a row of warehouses, Jack helped Fawn down the ramp and they all headed for town. It was a pleasant day, warm and humid, but not overly so. A mild breeze came off the bay with the accompanying scent of salt and fish. Seabirds were in the air and roosting on ropes and poles. The port city was a hum of activity. Cargo was being moved off and onto ships and in and out of warehouses. Dockworkers and seamen were most prevalent along the wharf, while townsfolk and immigrants, fresh from Europe, were more in evidence within the city streets.

The directions they had been given were simple. First, walk past the warehouses toward the city. Then, turn right by the fish market. At the next street, go left a half block.

The building that they were looking for was on the

left side, across the street from a gray restaurant fashioned with a nautical scheme. Jack could see that the smells from the cafe's kitchen were reminding Dan and Fawn of just how long it had been since they had last eaten. They were both staring across in the direction of The Whaler's Cafe and Bar as they neared the typically unadorned, green government building. Above its solid pine door in black letters was printed *Harbormaster.*

Just before they were about to step onto the boardwalk that lined the business fronts, Jack turned and stopped. He gave a slight motion with his head toward the cafe. "No point in you two tagging along with me. Why don't you order up something for us while I find out what's sailing for Mexico."

"I was hoping you'd say that, partner. Why—I'm hungry enough to eat that whale." Dan pointed to the carved, wooden blue whale that hung high above the restaurant's entrance, with the cafe's name written in script upon it.

With Jack's response of a smile and a single nod, they went their respective ways. It wasn't many minutes before his business with the harbormaster was completed and he, too, headed across the street toward the restaurant.

Just below the carved blue whale was the high point of a large rope that spanned the width of the establishment. From there the rope draped down beneath round, ship-style windows on both sides of the entry door. Jack passed through the mahogany door complete with brass fixtures, which looked like it had originally been from a ship's cabin, and looked around. The nautical theme continued inside. Assorted fish nets, shells, mounted fish, and anchors decorated the walls of the not very well-lit interior. Across the disarray of various sized and shaped tables was a kitchen and bar at the far left. There were a half dozen sea-toughs seated at a long table toward the back of the place on the right-hand side. It seemed to Jack that they must have been tipping the ale mugs for quite a while. Their voices were loud and laced with a sailor's vulgarity. He gave them a brief stare, not disguising his contempt, before looking left, where Fawn and Dan were sitting at a corner table up front.

As he walked to their table, his stern expression softened. They had been facing away from the obnoxious seamen, making an attempt to ignore them and were now looking back at Jack's approach. He stopped, managed a smile, bent down, and kissed Fawn lightly on the cheek. The romantic display was largely for the benefit of the swabs—a small gesture to let the drunks across the room know how things were before one of them decided to provoke something. However, he was growing very tired of their language. If they kept it up, he wondered, would he end up doing the provoking?

Jack then went around to the far side of their table so he could watch the men and, as always, keep his back to the wall. He settled into his chair. The six men were still spewing profanity with drunken abandon and were, if anything, even louder. He gave them another menacing stare and then turned to Fawn. "You want me to do something about that?"

She shook her head. "They don't bother me. They're just drunk."

"They bother me." He had that look. It was the look that would scare anyone who knew him or who he was. Jack McCall wasn't an easy man to get riled, but he lived by a code, the code of the West. There were things men weren't supposed to do in the presence of a female. He knew it and couldn't understand why they didn't. "There's no excuse for bad manners. Not in front of a lady." He stated it with simple conviction and added, "Maybe I should go over there and deal with those sea dogs."

Dan looked back at the uncouth salts and then back to his partner. "You can't kill 'em just for bein' louts, Jack."

His focus remained on the six men, but he gave a shake of the head. "Wasn't planning on killing them, Dan. But someone should straighten them out." He turned to Dan. "I'd just explain it to them in a very clear way. I think they'd stop."

"And what if they didn't?"

"Maybe I'd have to bust them up a bit," he smiled. "That's all. But it'd be for their own good. Just help them remember their manners."

Fawn leaned toward Jack and took his hand. She looked him gently in the eyes and spoke softly. "I know you feel like you have to protect me and right every wrong you see. But not this time. I'm not listening to a word they say and they're not worth the trouble."

He found himself nodding to the last few words. "All right, if that's the way you want it." He glanced once again at the six foul-mouthed drunks, then back to her. "There probably isn't time to right the world today, anyway."

"Does that mean you found something sailing to

Mexico?" She seemed relieved to get Jack's attention away from the sailors.

"Well, there just might be a ship for us today. It's named *Azteca.* It was here for repairs, but it's been moved from the shipyard. It's supposed to sail this afternoon, but they couldn't tell me if it was moved to another dock or at anchor in the bay."

At that moment, the six men started singing a song with particularly raunchy lyrics. Jack quickly pushed his chair back, stood up, and walked straight for the out of tune and irreverent choir. It happened fast enough that Dan and Fawn didn't immediately realize where he was heading. It was too late for words. All they could do was turn their chairs around to watch and exchange blank expressions.

Jack stopped a few feet from the seamen's table and gave each of the men a hard stare in turn. Their voices trailed off for a few seconds and then there was a brief silence.

The big man to the far left spoke first. His beard was full, like the others, but he wasn't so unkempt. The clothes he donned were similar to the blue-and-white nautical garb his cohorts also wore, except his were pressed and clean. He gave Jack a wary look. When he spoke, it was also apparent that he was less inebriated than the other five. "You looking for trouble, cowboy?"

"I can usually find that all by myself. In fact, it usually comes looking for me." It was said in an offhanded, even friendly way. He used his right hand to push his Stetson back on his head, a gesture aimed to ease tension. He then continued. "Actually I'm looking for a ship called *Azteca*. Any of you boys know where it's docked?"

To Jack's surprise, the men started laughing again. Perplexed, he glanced back at Dan and Fawn. His efforts in diplomacy seemed to have failed, and they could see that he was getting a little agitated. He turned back and glared at the same big man, who was doing his share of the laughing.

He could see that Jack's patience was running low and held up both hands in appeasement. His words then seemed to sputter through the laughter. "Don't get mad there, cowboy." He turned to his mates for a moment, then back to Jack. "We just thought it mighty funny that you'd ask us if we knew where our ship was."

"You're part of the *Azteca* crew?"

"Why, I'm the captain. She's my ship, cowboy." There was a certain amount of pride in the answer. He then gestured toward the other five men with him. "This here is about half her crew. She's not a big ship."

"You're going to Vera Cruz?"

"We're going a bit farther south than that, cowboy, but that's our next stop. Why?"

"The three of us would like to book passage with you, as far as Vera Cruz."

"Don't usually carry passengers, cowboy. She's a merchant ship." He motioned to the man on his left. "We'd have to boot my first mate, Billy here, out of his quarters to make room for you." As the man called Billy showed irritation in his expression, the captain leaned forward and looked up at Jack. "Don't like doing that to my friend. You'd have to make it worth my while, cowboy."

"How much?"

"A hundred—one hundred dollars, cowboy."

"Fifty." Jack wasn't about to pay that much.

"Seventy-five."

"Sixty."

The captain glanced at his first mate, then back to Jack. He gave a couple reluctant nods. "Looks like Billy's giving up his cabin." He got to his feet and stated, "Done." While he offered Jack his hand, he added, "The name's LeBoux. We're sailing on the afternoon tide. Bring the money."

Jack gave his name as he shook the captain's hand, but somehow didn't entirely trust the man.

Chapter 11
Azteca

The captain and crew waited for Jack and company to finish their meal and then led the way toward the docks. There was a small bookstore a half block from the cafe. Fawn dashed in, knowing a book or two would help the time pass during the voyage. The others waited outside for the couple of minutes it took for her to return with two Western novels and a science magazine. *A good choice,* Jack thought.

As they continued along their way, Captain LeBoux explained that they had a run-in with a tropical storm, two days out of New Orleans. That was the reason they docked in to Galveston Bay. It had done enough damage to the ship that it took three days to put it right. It was moved from the shipyard just that morning and was resting, at anchor, a few hundred yards out in the bay with several other ships. They were all waiting for the change of tide and wind to take them out to sea.

There was a longboat with two crewmen waiting

dockside. With all onboard, the two oarsmen pulled toward the *Azteca*. As they got closer, Jack studied the ship. He didn't know much about ships. In fact, Captain LeBoux had to tell him that it was a schooner. That meant it had a mainmast about in the middle of the ship, a foremast nearer the bow, and a jib all the way forward. Jack would have called it a derelict. It was black and no more than fifty-foot long. At one time it must have been a sleek—even pretty—vessel, but that was long ago. It appeared to have been neglected for some years. The black paint on the hull had peeled, faded, been rubbed off in numerous places, and had dark-green algae encrusted along the waterline. All the rigging and sail looked old and worn. He noticed makeshift repairs and patches wherever he looked. The only new part of the ship was the foremast. Jack figured it took quite a storm to break the old one. Near the top of the bow was the name *Azteca* in faded gold paint. At least that seemed a good omen.

Soon the longboat was brought alongside the *Azteca*, and a crewman topside dropped a rope ladder. A stout Mexican sailor offered a hand as each one neared the top deck and helped them aboard. The view topside was hardly appealing. It wasn't just a rundown ship, it was dirty. Jack reminded himself that it was a merchant ship, not intended for passengers, and the only one heading for Vera Cruz. He also considered it a lucky circumstance that the captain and crew happened to pick the same cafe as they did. Then he considered the men's behavior and the condition of the ship and wondered if lucky was the right word.

The first mate, Billy, was noticeably unhappy about

the three guests. Still, he gathered a couple crewmen, led them one deck below, and began moving his things out of his cabin.

Minutes after that work began, the breeze started to pick up. It shifted direction and began blowing southwest. As quickly as the wind arrived, the crew on deck began pulling in the anchor and making sail. The sails were hoisted both fore and main and instantly bulged out tight against the steady breeze. The ship's wheel was forward inside forecastle, and the helmsman began steering to port. Jack was impressed with the efficiency of the ragged-looking crew. The ship slowly gained speed and started making its way to the open sea.

Dan and Fawn seemed content to watch the crew swing into action, all knowing their job without being told. Jack was looking back at the city, docks, and ships moored. They were all growing smaller as the *Azteca* followed the channel out through the bay. Once the ship reached the open waters of the Gulf of Mexico, she sailed south-southwest, in calm seas and warm sultry breezes.

Ten days, more or less, was the sailing time to Vera Cruz, dependent upon the wind. That's how Captain LeBoux put it. A long time on a small ship in a cramped cabin.

The cabin was adequate for one man with a single cot in a confined space, but very tight for three. It was dimly lit and devoid of comforts. The air within their quarters was humid and musty.

Even if it wasn't the only space onboard for passengers, they would have stayed together. It just wasn't safe to leave Fawn by herself with the surly sailors about.

The swabs gave her the kind of looks that made her feel quite uncomfortable. So she didn't mind the odd accommodations or even Dan's snoring. In fact, she had come to think of the old-timer as the grandfather she never had, but didn't let him know it. She slept on the cot, leaving Dan and Jack to make-do on the floor.

They ended up spending much of the time up on deck, near the crew. Although they tried to stay out of the sailor's way, it was too small a craft to be by one's self for long.

The crew also tried to stay to themselves, perhaps on the captain's orders. Still Jack thought it odd that the same loud, raucous, talkative men from the cafe were now so quiet. *Why were they so different on liberty,* he wondered. *Was it that they simply tended to business while onboard, or did it have something to do with having passengers nearby?*

The answer came on the fourth day out. Both Dan and Fawn had something to tell Jack. They led him to the bow of the ship, beneath the small forward sail, which the sailors called a jib. It was midday, and all but three of the crew were below at the galley eating. Of those three, one was at the wheel and the other two were astern. It was one of the few times when they were certain not to be overheard. However, their place of meeting was not ideal. The swells were medium to heavy that day, so as the bow dipped down and plowed into the upcoming swell, there was a loud crashing sound with accompanying spray. They huddled together on the deck and spoke while riding atop the swells, and held tight to the anchor chain when the bow plunged down.

"So what did you two have on your minds?"

Dan motioned for her to go first.

She was visibly upset. "I just went down to our cabin to get a different book and caught the first mate going through our things. He stumbled out something about looking for a missing chart, but that was a lie. He was rifling through everything we have."

"Probably looking for money, don't you think?"

She simply shrugged and then paused, waiting for the crash and spray to subside. She wiped the salty water from her eyes and turned to Dan. "Tell him what you heard, Dan."

He used his sleeve to dry his face and then began. "Early this mornin' around daybreak, I was comin' up top to get some air. There were two fellers from the crew already up there talkin' and didn't know I was there. So I stopped halfway up the ladder and listened. These ain't merchant sailors, Jack. They're gunrunners. It ain't rice and cotton down in the hold like they said; it's rifles for some banditos below the Yucatan Peninsula."

Jack put his right hand over his eyes, while holding on to the anchor chain with his left, as he rode out another plunge and shower. He blinked a little from the salt. "I don't see where there's much that we can do about it right now."

"Ain't like you to let something like this go, partner." Dan seemed disappointed.

"We need these pirates to sail the ship. I'll deal with them when we get to Mexico."

"Good. Thought you were goin' soft there for a second." There was a smile on his wet face.

Fawn shook her head. "Listen to you two. Did we come down here to fight pirates or find that island?"

Jack just smiled.

"Let the Mexican police or army take care of this," Fawn continued. "Besides, I doubt if they'd appreciate you doing their job in their country."

Jack leaned over to her and kissed her salty cheek. "All right, we'll do it your way. After all, you're always right. In the meantime, Dakota and I will take turns sleeping, and we'll stick close together."

They both nodded.

Chapter 12
Vera Cruz

Six days later, the *Azteca* sailed into Puerto de Vera Cruz. The crew quickly dropped and secured the mainsail. The ship slipped past the island lighthouse, which looked like a castle fortress, built upon an island within the bay. The domed lighthouse sat at the very top of the huge structure and was already sending a beam out across the sea.

It was dusk and lights began to appear throughout the city. Vera Cruz was an old city, with classic Spanish-Mediterranean architecture. It was built right up to the seawall and, as seen from shipboard, was quite beautiful. There were ships out in the harbor at anchor, and many at their moorings along the docks.

Under halfsail, and a very light breeze, the schooner turned to port and slowly eased past the line of ships docked at the city's edge. There was an open berth ahead and the crew moved to bring her in. They dropped the foresail as the helmsman then turned to starboard. The *Azteca* was nearly stopped by the maneuver and at the same time brought the bow in close enough for the crew to toss a couple lines to men on shore. In a matter of minutes, she was being tied off and the gangway was lowered.

The three passengers quietly left the ship. The past six days had gone by without incident or alarm. They had stayed to themselves and watched one another's back. It seemed that the crew was just as happy to see them go as they were to leave the vessel. The captain remained courteous, although it didn't seem entirely genuine. He had mentioned that he would let the crew stay in port for two days before continuing south. Jack hoped their stay would be much longer, taking up residence in a Mexican prison.

The first thing on their minds was to find a hotel. Next, they would talk to the police. It wasn't long before they found a suitable hotel. It was just a block from the docks and related shipping businesses. A signpost led them up a narrow, cobbled street to *Hotel Serenidad*. A series of brick arches over smooth adobe walls made up the front exterior facade. At the far right, the archway's adobe was replaced by two dark oak doors. They were open and behind them was the office and front desk. The man behind the desk was probably no more than forty. He was small, thin, and wore a friendly smile.

Jack led the way into the hotel lobby and returned the smile. "*Buenos noches, señor.*"

"*Buenos noches.*" He leaned over the desk and gave all the same smile. "My name is Javier Lopez. This is my hotel. How can I be of service?"

"Well, we'd like a room for three." Jack still had LeBoux and his crew on his mind. He wasn't about to leave Fawn alone.

"*Bueno, señor.* I have just what you want, number four. Seven pesos a night." He pointed down the hallway.

Jack nodded. "Fine. But I'm curious. Where'd you learn your English. It sure is a lot better than my Spanish."

He slid the hotel register and pen closer for Jack to sign. As he did so, he answered. "I went north when I was fifteen. A couple years ago, I ended up prospecting outside of Tombstone. I found enough silver to come back here and buy this hotel."

"Small world," Jack added. "We just came from Arizona."

After Señor Lopez glanced at the new name on his register, he seemed to be giving Jack a hard, serious stare. Then the smiled returned. "I know you, Mr. McCall." He looked down at Jack's guns and the smile grew wider. "I saw you in Bisbee, in the show." He shook his head. "*Muy rapido,* I couldn't believe it."

Jack reached across, and they shook hands over the counter. He always appreciated his audience. "It's just Jack, to my *amigos.*"

"It's an honor, Jack." He seemed a little overwhelmed. "It's Javier to you and your friends and if there's anything you need, just ask."

"We do need to report something to the *policia.* Where would we find them?"

"*Si.* Not far. Go two blocks into town." He pointed to his right. "Then, turn left. The *Estacion de Policia* is there, next to the *Oficina de Postal.*"

"*Muchas gracias,* Javier."

Javier then pulled the key from the wall behind him and handed it to Jack. With one last gracias, they went to the room to drop off their bedrolls.

Minutes later they stood inside the smallish police station. There was but one officer on duty, a stout and rather stern-looking hombre, with a full moustache and sergeant's uniform. He sat behind a flat-topped desk, looking impatient. Jack watched as he was taking statements and trying to sort out a dispute between the two men before him. They both believed the other owed him money.

It didn't look like it would be their turn soon since the two men before the sergeant were equally convinced that they were right. While Jack seemed amused by it all, Fawn was bored by the bickering and started looking around the small office. She found herself looking at the many wanted posters tacked to every inch of open wall space. Suddenly, her eyes got very wide and she heard herself gulp. She instantly went up behind Jack and spun him around. Looking up at him and pulling him as close as possible, she whispered, "Don't turn around, and don't say anything. Just come outside. Now!"

Jack's expression was very puzzled, but he did as he was told. She led him out the door, took his hand, and pulled him a little ways down the street from the police station. When they stopped, she noticed that Dan was right behind them. She gave a little scan from side to side to be sure they were alone and then spoke softly. "There's a wanted poster in there." She looked right at Jack. "You're wanted in Nogales for murder! There's a ten-thousand-peso reward on you."

Jack's face seemed to go blank. He turned to Dan as it slowly started to make some sense in his mind. "Those two bushwhackers."

Dan nodded. "I bet Foley had somethin' to do with this. That low-down snake. He probably said he saw the whole dang thing and put up the reward money."

"Guess he found his revenge."

"What are you two talking about?" She gave Jack a serious look. "Did you really kill somebody in Nogales?"

"Man named Foley with two hired guns came after me in Nogales. I just winged Foley, but the other two tried to dry-gulch me. Had to kill the both of them."

"So why didn't you give the police your side of it?"

It seemed that Dan didn't like her having the wrong idea about his partner and spoke up. "Heck, it weren't none of Jack's fault. We would have squared him with the law, but there weren't no time. He had to high-tail it back to save those two boys."

"I did make one mistake. I took their rifles."

"You got a right to take the gun a man tries to kill you with, partner. It's always been like that. Code of the West."

"It seemed fair enough at the time, but it must have made it look like they were unarmed."

Fawn was visibly relieved. "I'm sorry. I know what kind of man you are. You did what you had to do." She put her arms up, and he lifted her up by the waist while she wrapped her arms around his neck.

Jack set her down easy, and she glanced back at the police station. "Well, we've got to avoid the police. You're not going to some Mexican jail."

Dan nodded. "She's right, partner. You and I can go

back to Nogales and straighten this out later. I've got a little pull in that town. I helped the *federales* a time or two when I was a deputy." He shook his head. "You sure don't want to get arrested down here!"

"All right. We'll stay clear of police and pirates until we finish what we came here for. But I don't like letting those gunrunners get away."

"One thing at a time, sweetheart." She took him by the hand. "Let's go get some sleep. There's an island out there waiting for us."

Chapter 13
Jack's Design

Fawn stirred from her slumber and glanced around the room's spartan white-brick interior. A single window near the door supplied the only source of daylight. Their quarters were furnished with three narrow beds and a small table, complete with pitcher and wash basin. Dan was still sleeping, noisily, in the far bed by the wall. The bed in between was empty, with the one plaid blanket thrown aside. Jack had quietly slipped out some time during the night or morning. She wondered when and why.

Feeling a little anxious, she roused Dan out of bed. "Did you see Jack leave?"

Still drowsy, he came to his feet, rubbing his eyes. After a couple of yawns, he finally seemed to wake up a little and shook his head. "Sorry, Fawn. I slept right through." He started to show a troubled expression. "Why would he take off without us?"

She ran her fingers through her hair and twitched her

mouth into a frown. "I don't know about that man sometimes. A wanted poster hanging over his head and he wanders off without so much as a word." She started for the door and looked back. "Come on, let's find him."

It took some effort for Dan just to keep up. She headed back in the direction of the docks. When she turned right toward the *Azteca*, Dan, slightly out of breath, wheezed out, "Hold on a second!"

She spun around and snapped, "What?"

"Where the heck are we goin'?"

"To find Jack before he gets into trouble."

"Can't imagine any trouble he'd get into that he couldn't just as easily get out of." He said it like she should have already known it. "And what makes you think he's gonna be around here?"

"You heard him last night. We can't go to the police, but he doesn't want those gunrunners to get away." She put her hands on her hips. "He probably thought he could take care of the whole crew and be back before breakfast."

"I wouldn't bet against it, but he didn't."

"How do you know that?"

"Because he told you he wouldn't."

Dan could see the tension in her eyes begin to fade. She looked down and then slowly back to Dan. She almost seemed ashamed. "Then where is he?"

"Don't know, but he'd never go back on his word. Especially not to you."

"Those pirates and that wanted poster have given me the jitters." She put her hand under his scruffy chin and smiled. "Thanks, Dan. I should have known better."

She gave him a look tinged with remorse. "Please don't tell Jack that I doubted him."

He shook his head. "Course not."

They turned and headed back along the docks for the hotel. As they did so, the tall, dark silhouette of Jack McCall could be seen a block or so ahead. He had just passed the shipyard. When he saw who was coming, he picked up the pace.

They met adjacent to a red brick and adobe cantina. Fawn couldn't entirely hide that she had been concerned about him. "And where have you been?"

Jack sensed a little tension, smiled, and motioned toward the cantina. "Let's go in here and I'll tell you what I've been up to."

It was a quaint little dockside bar and cafe called *Los Equipales*, named for the type of wicker furniture that decorated its interior. There was a kitchen behind the bar all the way in the back left corner. Arched windows graced the cafe's front, allowing a view of the bay. The six round tables were in no particular order. All the chairs had wide oval backs, a part of the equipales style. They settled into the far right table.

After the cafe's owner—who doubled as waiter and bartender—had taken their order for breakfast, Jack gazed fondly at his sweetheart. "Had some business to get started early, but didn't want to wake you. It took a bit longer than planned."

"What sort of business?" She had lost any sign of sharpness in her tone.

"I had to get things underway for our little expedition. The sailboat was easy. I hired one for eleven o'clock this morning. But I had to have a couple things made. That's why I had to get an early start."

Dan's eyes revealed his curiosity. "What kind of things, partner?"

"Well, I've been thinking about how we're going to find that island and how I could stay underwater for a long time."

Fawn leaned forward. "I've got to hear this."

Jack smiled. "It's not that clever. Fortunately, there's all kinds of tradesman and shops along this harbor. You tell these Mexicans what you want, wave enough pesos in front of their noses, and they'll make it for you. And pronto."

"Okay, they're making it, and you don't think it's clever. But what is it?" Curiosity was getting the best of her.

"Alright." He was enjoying their inquisitive nature. "First, there's a cabinetmaker building a glass-bottomed box. It's open at the top and will float. When we get close enough, I'll look through the glass to see deeper below the ocean's surface."

Fawn gave Dan a glance and nod before prodding, "And what else?"

"Well, you two remember what I used for air in the cave?"

They both nodded.

"I knew that wouldn't work this time, it won't hold enough air. Besides, if I carried it with me while trying to swim down, the thing would want to lift me back up to the surface. So I'm having a larger bag made with hooks, ropes, and a small basket attached."

"I don't follow you." Dan seemed to speak for both of them.

"Well, the air bag they're making is about two foot across and will look a lot like one of those French hot-air balloons. You know, with ropes going down to a basket, but in this case, the basket's just to hold rocks for ballast. It'll take some weight to keep the air bag below the surface. And there will be one long rope between the air bag and the anchor basket that I can lengthen or shorten to keep the bag of air at the right depth."

There was something of a gleam in Fawn's eyes. "So the spout would be pointing down, so the air wouldn't escape."

"Well, there's a plug in the spout."

"Of course, it's under pressure. So, you swim over to it, take out the plug, and after you've filled your lungs, replace it to save the air."

He nodded.

"Then it's just making sure that the rope is adjusted so the bag is close to you."

"Yeah, pretty much. But I'm not sure how much pressure there will be if I have to go very deep.

"You're right. The deeper you go, the greater the compression."

"That's why I had them make the spout out of rubber with a tapered cork plug in it. That way I can pinch it off and control the air if there's a lot of pressure on the bag."

"But you don't think that's clever." There was a hint of sarcasm in her words."

Jack shrugged. "Ask me again if it works."

Moments later the proprietor arrived with breakfast. They took their time. There was no hurry, with nearly three hours to kill. They whiled away much of that time there, in the cantina. It was a pleasant place to wait. After eating they sipped their coffee and looked out toward the bay. All manner of people passed by, even two crewmen from the *Azteca*. Fawn saw Jack's eyes tighten up at their presence.

After a couple hours, they moseyed back to the hotel. Fawn retrieved the map of Mexico from her bedroll, while Jack told Javier that they would be there at least another night. He was as friendly and gracious as before.

It was getting close enough to 11:00 A.M. to head out. Along the way they picked up a hammer and chisel and two extra lengths of rope from a hardware store. The cabinetmaker had the glass-bottom box finished when they got there, and Dan was designated to carry it. The leather bag was also done. The leather shop had just finished it, had filled it with water, and was checking it for leaks. Jack gave it his own inspection and was satisfied.

The bag was drained as Jack checked to see if the ropes were done to his design. Simple, really. There was a long rope that had a slipknot so he could adjust its length. Four small ropes were used to attach the air bag and ballast basket to each end of that long, adjustable rope. They would pick up ballast rocks to put in the basket along the way.

With ropes hanging heavy around his neck and shoulders and carrying the leather bag upside down to let the rest of the water drip out, Jack bid his constructors adios. He then led the way down to the dock where he rented the boat and wondered if it would all actually work.

Chapter 14
A Whole Lot Of Water

It was a sixteen-foot skiff. Jack thought it looked a lot like a rowboat, but with a single sail and rudder. The small craft was tied off to a slip, a little ways out. He could see, looking at Dan and Fawn, that they wished it was a bigger boat. The reason he rented that particular boat was because there simply wasn't anything else. Besides, he figured, with what he knew about boats the smaller the better. He also liked the fact that it had oars. If he couldn't get it to go where he wanted by sail, he would simply use his muscles.

Of course the owner of the skiff, and five boats just like it, assumed that Jack had sailed before. Jack didn't mention that this would be his first time. As Jack counted out the pesos for one day's rent, the owner mentioned that there might be some weather coming from the east in a day or two. It seemed that a steamer came into port a few hours earlier. It had out run a storm off Cuba. Jack bid him gracias and then looked out to sea. The sky was blue and the wind was mild. That storm might not even get this far, he figured. Besides, one day should be enough.

They walked down the slip and piled all the gear forward. Then Dan and Fawn stepped down into the back of the rocking boat. Once settled in, Dan held on to the wooden slip while Jack untied both lines and got down into the middle seat. They pushed off away from the slip, and Jack grabbed the oars. He pulled away from the docks and out into the bay. Soon they were midway into the bay channel.

Dan watched him working with the oars and finally looked to Fawn. "How far did you say it was to where we're headed?"

"I think it's about fifteen miles or so."

He turned back to Jack, who was still working pretty hard. "You plan on rowin' the whole way, partner? You know this thing has a sail?"

Jack laid the oars across his lap and took a couple deep breaths. "I thought it would be a good idea to get way out in the bay before I tried to figured out how to use the sail."

Dan's eyes narrowed. "You mean to tell me you've never done this before?"

"Nope. Have you?"

"Heck, Jack. I never even saw the ocean before we got on that merchant ship."

Jack looked behind him at the eight-foot-high mast, with its sail and boom still tied secure, and then back to his partner. "I know you're supposed to let the wind do the work. I just don't know how yet."

As Dan rolled his eyes, Fawn casually added, "I know how."

"You've sailed before?" Jack seemed quite surprised.

"I didn't say that, but I've read about it. It's called tack. To position the sail at the right angle against the wind." She smiled. "It's simple. You can go anywhere except straight into the wind. So sometimes you have to zigzag to get where you're going."

"Go on, teacher." Jack didn't really mind the lesson.

She held up her hand to feel the breeze. "Like right now, the wind's going north-northwest. It's blowing from behind us and a little to the left. But think of the boat as a clock, with the point of the bow being twelve o'clock. See how the wind is coming from about four o'clock and across to ten o'clock. In this case, the sail should be about straight back."

That was enough for Jack. He untied the ropes around the mast and let the boom down easy. Fawn secured the boom to port and starboard with two ropes tied to the appropriate rings, positioning it parallel with the craft. Then she unfurled the sail. It puffed out full, causing the boat to lean over to port about fifteen degrees as it slowly started to gain speed. She steered a little to starboard to compensate for the opposing wind, and they were sailing. Soon she had to turn the boat to starboards, to go around the island lighthouse. Fawn needed to let the sail swing around farther to port. So she slackened the right hand rope to the boom and shortened the left one and then steered right. The sail flapped around until she finished the turn, but then flared out tight again. They were headed out to sea.

Jack, looking suitably impressed, asked, "You can do this just from reading a book?"

She nodded. "You'd be surprised what you can get from a book. Even that science magazine I just bought. There's all kinds of interesting things in it."

"You see, Dan, we're being left behind. I think we'd better go back to school."

"No thanks, it didn't take the first time. Guess I'll let you two do the thinkin' around here."

Once they cleared the bay, she turned the boat north. They stayed a few miles offshore. That was something else from her book on sailing. If you don't know the coastline, it's safer to stay in deep water. There could be reefs, snags, and strong currents closer to shore.

The wind was in their favor, a steady breeze blowing northwest. It was carrying them along at about six knots. The sea had mild swells and was crystal clear. To their left was a lush, green coast. The jungle often bordered the rugged shoreline and beaches. A few fishing camps could be seen, with long, white fishing boats pulled onto the beaches. The boats were resting there until the tiny fleets went to sea the next morning.

Fawn continued to navigate up the coast for a couple more hours. There was another fish camp coming up. It had a wide sandy beach. They headed in, dropping the sail as they approached, letting the tide take them in.

The boat slid onto the white-sand beach bow first. Jack then jumped out and pulled it far enough up the beach that the returning tide wouldn't carry her back out.

He made a quick survey of the area. Straight ahead the jungle met the beach. Far to the left was a rocky hillside that jutted out into the sea. Loose stones were scattered along its base. Those stones would be useful. On the opposite end of the beach, he noted a group of fishermen way back near the jungle behind their boats. There were a dozen or so fishermen cleaning their catch on a long table beneath a palapa. Pelicans were snatching up every scrap tossed to them in seconds. Gulls circled overhead, waiting for their chance.

Jack sent Dan to gather the stones that would be used for ballast, while he spoke to the fishermen. For a few pesos, they were happy to supply lunch. The resourceful Mexicanos quickly made a sand pit, picked up some loose wood from the jungle, and made a fire. Minutes later they were cooking dorado on makeshift skewers. The fish was quite good.

It wasn't long before Jack was rowing the skiff away from the beach against the tide and into deeper water. Fawn then took over as they continued to sail north. Within a mile they could see a fair-sized pueblo. It was a pretty Spanish colonial town, carved out of the jungle. Nestled between the sea, a river, and the jungle, it made for a picturesque setting. A sleepy little village of small adobe homes surrounded the town center, which had a Moorish theme of domed roofs.

They sailed right past the village of Zempoala. Ahead they could see the entrance to a river. Jack pointed in the direction of 2:00, and Fawn steered that way. They headed for the horizon until they could just see landfall and where the river met the sea.

Jack dropped the sail and secured the boom up in place to make more room. Dan was looking all around and wore a doubtful expression. "So what happens now, partner?"

"This is where I get wet, Dakota."

"I know, but there's a whole passel of water out there. What makes you think we're in the right spot?"

"I expect it's going to take some looking, but it's not exactly a needle in a haystack."

Fawn gave a nod. "You see, Dan, we have a cross reference."

Dan shrugged, not understanding.

"Well, that old story written down by the priest said the island was directly off a river. It also told of a reflection on the horizon at sundown. Well, that's pretty much where we are."

Jack took off his hat, vest, boots, and gunbelt. He then removed the money from his pocket and dropped it into his left boot, while adding, "Besides, we're not looking for a needle. That island was big enough to build a pyramid on it. I should be able to find it."

Dan once again looked full circle and shrugged. "You two are the thinkers around here. Just looks like a whole lot of water to me."

Chapter 15
Island Lost

Dan took Jack's place in the middle seat to man the oars as Jack slipped into the water. Fawn then passed him the glass-bottomed box. It had been constructed fairly shallow, so he was able to use the box as a float, pulling himself up just high enough to see over the side and down into the glass. That allowed him to see deep into the crystal-clear water, but also saved him some energy. He didn't have to tread water, but just kicked his feet enough to keep moving.

Fawn kept him on track. From her position in the boat, she could make sure that he was going in a straight pattern, not making circles or covering the same area. She would have him go north until he reached a point adjacent to a prominent hill at landfall. Then she had him move out farther away from shore and then return south. It was a slow and careful method, traveling back and forth, gradually moving out to sea.

If the story was at all accurate, they would find the island that way. If it wasn't, there was no chance anyway.

Jack continued to hunt. Dan kept the boat close behind. Hours passed and frustration settled in. Those in the boat were weary of the sun and humidity. The man in the water was getting discouraged.

It was late afternoon. Time and light was running out. What Jack saw below was not what he expected. It was a very uneven bottom, mostly sandy, with the occasional dark rock of all sizes here and there. Somehow he thought there would be some sort of clues. He figured there might be the outline of an island, or maybe some man-made stones. He even thought the island could be fairly close to the surface. Instead there was a sameness. An undulating ocean floor covered with white sand that stretched out in all directions and the occasional sea life.

His mind began to doubt the whole venture. As he considered how he had brought Dan and Fawn so far only to find sand, he started moving faster. It wasn't desperation, but he did feel a certain amount of urgency. He also felt a slight change in the wind. It was cooler and had shifted a little; it was now blowing west. If a storm was on its way, then time was running short. Jack also didn't like to fail at anything, but the thought of letting those in the boat down was even worse. He brushed aside any doubts and pressed on.

He continued on the present southerly course, but at an accelerated speed. Soon he was breathing pretty hard. Still he stubbornly went on, straining his eyes for the smallest clue. He was getting toward the end of that southern leg. Then, just as Fawn was about to direct him to the make the next turn, he suddenly saw a dark shape from the corner of his eye a ways out to sea. He instantly turned that way and kicked even harder. His heart was beating harder and faster. It was partly because he was using a lot of energy, but also because he saw what they had come for. Growing larger before him was a formation that could be nothing other than a pyramid.

Jack stopped just above the sunken temple. He gazed down on it while trying to catch his breath. Not surprisingly, it was covered with marine encrustations and a dark green blanket of moss. Jack guessed the outer layer was plankton, or algae. The green moss covered every inch of the majestic structure, but that didn't hide its beauty. Although not as large as the ones on the mainland, it was a classic pyramid design. The four triangular sides that pointed to the top were made of stone blocks. On the north wall was a narrow stairway that traveled about midway up the wall to what might be called a landing. It was a fair-sized stone platform and just beyond it was an opening that was apparently the entrance. The four walls terraced up to a square stone that capped the structure. Upon that top stone was what looked like a round vertical disk. It was, he was quite sure, what they had come for. Like all the rest of the temple, it was covered with green moss on top of sea encrustations. He would soon know if it was really made of gold.

Jack turned back to the skiff, still using the glass-bottomed box as a float. His grin gave away the news, but he told them anyway. "We're right over it."

"How deep is it?" Fawn seemed more interested in the dangers than the object they had come for.

"I'm not too good at judging distance through water. But I don't think it's too far to swim down. I'm sure I can get it. That bag of air should help, though."

Dan couldn't hide his excitement. His face was beaming. "Could you see it, Jack? Could you see the gold sun?"

"It's there. Right on top. Of course, it's green."

Dan's face dropped. "Green?"

"Don't let that worry you, Dan." Fawn's voice was reassuring. "It's just a part of being in seawater so long." Then she shrugged. "On the other hand, it could be made of bronze."

Dan didn't seem to like that answer. He looked at Jack. "I guess there's one way to find out."

Jack nodded. "Yeah, and we're running out of light." He gave a glance at the seaward horizon. "And I don't like the look of that sky." Far to the east was a gathering of dark clouds. Time was definitely not on their side.

They immediately began preparing for Jack's watery descent. Fawn first removed the plug from the air bag spout and then pulled against the leather on both sides of the bag to let air in. She then put the rubber spout in her mouth and inflated it the rest of the way. While she was doing that, the two men were busy with the ropes. The two extra ropes were tied to the long, adjustable rope, about midway between the air bag and the basket containing rocks. Fawn passed Jack the two tools he would need. He put the chisel in his left pocket and slipped the hammer under his belt. He then carefully positioned the boat over the intended area. Dan then eased the anchor basket over the side. He let out the rope, hand over hand, until he got to the bag of air. Then he grabbed hold of the other two ropes and let them out the rest of the way. Jack watched the basket through the glass box as it made its way to the level spot just before the temple's entrance.

The three ropes each had a purpose. Of course the main rope was attached to the air bag, which was by then suspended below the surface. Of the other two ropes, one was to keep the boat from drifting. The last one was more optimistic. It was to haul up their golden prize once Jack chiseled it free.

Fawn secured the two ropes to the skiff. She made sure that the anchor rope was snug and left the other one with plenty of play. With that completed, they were ready. Words seemed unnecessary and a waste of time; Jack simply took in several deep breaths and dived. Once below the leather bag of air, which was just a few feet down, he used the rope to speed his descent. With every handful of rope, he pulled himself deeper. When he reached the slipknot, which was there to adjust the air bag depth, he wound his right foot into the rope below him to keep from floating up and began lowering the bag. When the bag was a dozen or so feet above the golden sun, Jack stopped and tied off the rope. He could see that the water pressure at that depth was compressing the bag. It seemed risky to bring it lower. Too much pressure could blow out the plug and the bag would be flat and useless. Besides, at that moment, he really needed some air. It was time for a test.

He used the rope to assist his ascent and reached the bag in seconds. After pinching off the rubber spout and palming the plug, he released the kinked spout just enough for the test. Air bubbled out in a rush. The pressure on the bag made the air come out in a hurry. It only made sense, but he had to be sure before exhaling. He had to know his little devise would work. Jack blew out the stale air that was burning his lungs and put the spout in his mouth. It was a slightly tricky procedure. That kind of pressure could hurt his lungs if not controlled. He let the air in slowly, even though he needed it right away.

After a couple breaths from the bag, he returned the plug and looked down. He could see the gold sun atop the pyramid. He wasn't right over it, but directly above the steps that led to the temple's entrance. As he looked down, he noticed that from his jostling around on the rope the anchor basket had slid a couple feet to the side toward the outside steps. One more tug would knock it down a step or maybe even set it bouncing a few more. Either way Jack needed to do something about that.

He carefully pulled himself down to the heavy basket without causing it to slide farther toward the steps. As he started dragging it back away from the steps and toward the entrance, he was able to see a little ways into the temple. The light grew dim inside. More than about six feet inside was pure darkness. Still he made a quick survey. After one step down, the floor seemed to level out. It was littered with stones and other debris, all difficult to identify owing to the thick covering of green moss. Had he more time, it would have been interesting to poke around inside, but he didn't. He slid the weighted basket down behind the step inside, knowing it wouldn't be easy to dislodge from there.

Just as he got the bag in place, he noticed something odd a few feet within. It almost looked like a small snake. Of course it was green like everything else, but it lay upon the floor in a serpentine shape. It tantalized Jack and he just had to investigate. Putting the golden prize above on hold for a moment or two, he reached in far enough to pick it up. Because the object was nestled among the rest of the clutter, he hadn't seen the whole thing. As he picked it up, even though its true color was hidden, he knew it was a gold necklace. The round pendant connected to it was an even bigger surprise.

From the landing to the stone capping the smallish pyramid was no more than fifteen feet. Jack slid the necklace into his pants pocket and headed for the top. It was time to get to work. Between the hammer, chisel, and necklace, he had lost most of his buoyancy. The added weight made it easy to stay down and that saved him some energy. The disk was close to three feet across and was attached to the top stone, which was square in shape. There were two smaller stones, with a downward arch on top on either side and beneath the sun. They formed the base, with mortar holding it in place. Not wanting to damage the object he had come for, he decided to work on the mortar underneath the stone, keeping the chisel a safe distance from the precious, soft metal.

He braced his knees under the disk and began the effort. The water slowed the speed of the hammer, so there wasn't the same force as usual. It took time and that meant several trips to the air bag. He continued, with fading light, until he finally managed to split the mortar, which caused the stone to break free of the disk at the same time. He was then able to begin gently rocking the disk back and forth until it broke free of the stone behind it.

After laying the heavy piece carefully down, he went back to the bag for air. There was little time left. Light was fading fast. He took one more breath before he made his way down for the third rope. He untied that rope and went back to the disk. It was so dark at that point that he had to lace the rope around the disk entirely by feel.

With the job complete, he discarded the heavy hammer and chisel and swam to the rope, then up for the skiff. He emerged breathing heavily, right beside the boat. Stretching upward first with his right hand, then the left, he managed to grasp the side of the boat and started to pull himself up. He expected to see smiles from Fawn and Dan. They were there, but they weren't smiling. On the other side of the skiff, in the last moments of twilight, was an unwelcome sight. The dark and ominous shape of the *Azteca*. About twelve of the crew stood on the edge of the deck looking down at Jack. They all held rifles pointed his way.

Chapter 16
Dark Escape

Apparently Captain LeBoux and his pirates had just arrived. The *Azteca*'s sails were down and still being secured. The skiff's bow line was in the hands of a crewman and the two vessels were being brought together.

Jack at this point had his arms upon the skiff's railing and he was holding himself chest high with the boat. Dan and Fawn were nervously sitting together astern. Fawn was on Jack's side, just to his left, and was visibly shaking. He gave her his best reassuring smile before assessing his rivals.

It was twilight, with a fading purple and gray sunset silhouetting the dark ship. The *Azteca*'s deck was directly above him. He first made a quick study from side to side of the line of rifles aimed down at him. Then, with a glance inside the skiff, he realized his own guns were gone. When he looked back up at the ship, the captain was moving into view at the deck side. LeBoux stood looking bold, confident, and wearing Jack's holster.

Jack glanced Dan's way and his partner dropped his head a little before speaking. "They made me toss everything up to them. He's got your hat and boots. He's got my gun too. There was just too dang many guns to argue the point."

Jack answered with a nod and then looked back up at LeBoux. The captain gave a wily smile as he looked down at him. He then gestured for Jack to come up out of the water.

Jack lifted himself up and swung his legs in with one smooth motion. Once inside, he settled close beside Fawn and Dan and looked back up at LeBoux.

The captain seemed to be enjoying the moment. Getting the drop on a man like Jack McCall was something worth savoring. As he spoke, he retained the smile while sounding casual and arrogant. "Thanks for the guns, McCall." He pulled them out, studied them for a moment and then aimed them at Jack. "They sure are pretty."

"They'd look a lot better turned around the other way." He gave Leboux's crew another glance. "But as long as I'm being so generous, why don't I come up there and give you and your men a lesson on their use."

"That won't be necessary, cowboy."

"Then what do you want, Leboux?"

"Oh, I think you know."

Jack shrugged. Of course there was little doubt of what LeBoux had come for, but he wasn't about to give anything away.

"We've been keeping an eye on you. When you sailed north out of the harbor, we knew you'd end up somewhere around here. So we stayed out just beyond the horizon and watched." He pointed up to the crow's nest. "Took you some time before you ended up here. But you've been in this spot for quite a while." His eyes narrowed and his voice became serious. "You found it, didn't you, cowboy!"

"Found what?" Jack could do little but stall and run out the daylight. He considered his options. There weren't many.

"Don't play dumb, cowboy. You haven't been out here diving for oysters. We all know the legend of *Isla De Illuminada* and the golden sun. Of course, until my first mate found that map you had in your cabin, I didn't take it too seriously."

As Fawn realized that her offhanded scribbling of the island's name on that map had caused their present predicament, she looked painfully to Jack. He did his best to console her with a smile.

As LeBoux watched the tender moment between Jack and Fawn, he could see Jack's weak spot. "Alright, cowboy, no more talk. Either you give me the gold sun or I'm taking the girl."

It took no thought on Jack's part. He turned around, grabbed the rope, and braced his feet against the side of the boat. It took a few minutes for him to pull the heavy object to the surface. At that point, Dan and Fawn reached over the side to help bring it aboard. Jack then whispered softly to them both. "Keep an eye on me. When I give you the nod, we're going back over the side. So grab onto my clothes, we're going down fast. And remember, you've got to breath out through your nose and in with your mouth on that air bag."

Jack knew that once they were of no more use to the captain they would be killed. His plan was simple and desperate, but he could think of no other. Dan and Fawn also sensed that Leboux would leave no witnesses and understood Jack's plan.

With the heavy green disk within the skiff, Jack then tossed the loose end of its rope up to LeBoux. The captain then got a couple members of his crew to haul it up onto the *Azteca*'s deck.

In that moment, the crew's eyes were on the disk and their attention was consumed with one question. Was gold beneath the moss and encrustations? Jack could see that there would be no better chance. He gave his signal, clasped a firm grip on Fawn's and Dan's arms, and helped pull them over the side with him. Jack dived straight down with Dan and Fawn holding tightly to his pants and shirt. He quickly found and got hold of the anchor rope and used it to speed the descent while all three kicked furiously.

There was, luckily, a slight delay in reaction aboard the *Azteca*. LeBoux, using a knife, had just scraped the edge of the disk down to the shiny yellow metal. Although he heard the splash, it took just a moment to pull his attention away from his prize. By the time he ordered the crew to fire, Jack and company had managed to gain a little depth. A volley of fire opened up on the skiff. The crew must have thought their quarry were hiding behind it. In seconds, it was riddled with bullet holes. The firing continued randomly into the sea for over a minute. Some rounds had gotten close. The sound of bullets whizzing through the water all around you is as terrifying as anything. Pelting sounds were heard as the projectiles penetrated the surface, followed by the whooshing sound as they rushed by. Jack felt the concussion of one of the first bullets as it passed by his ear. Most weren't quite that close. Then as they continued the descent, they were out of range.

Soon Jack felt the knot connecting the anchor rope to the long adjustable rope. He instantly grabbed the long rope with his left hand, pulled out his knife with his right, and cut the anchor line free. This, unknown to the captain and crew, would set what was left of the skiff and the *Azteca* adrift. By that time, Jack was in serious need of air. He knew his two companions in tow would need it even more. He made his way quickly up to the air bag. It was a two-handed operation, so he twirled his right leg into the rope to stop from drifting up. Once he had kinked the spout and palmed the plug, he put his hand behind Fawn's neck and directed her mouth to the spout. She was just short of panic at that point, but her clear thinking and trust in Jack kept her in control. After two breaths, Jack brought Dan up the same way. Dan having a rather large chest could hold his breath quite a while. He was fairly calm under the circumstances, and got through the drill well. Jack then took his turn. And so it went, in rotation, for six very long minutes.

There were a couple things in their favor. It was getting darker above and the wind and currents would cause the *Azteca* to be carried along with them. They just had to wait long enough for the ship to drift away.

Jack sensed that Dan and Fawn had reached their limit. Not many could have controlled their fears in the ink-black depths as long as they had. They were also running out of air. Jack knew it was time. Using his knife, he reached down and cut the rope, freeing them of their anchor basket below. The air bag was largely depleted, but it still helped their ascent. They floated up and finally bobbed to the surface. As the others gasped for air, Jack turned full circle in search for the *Azteca*. In the distance, silhouetted before the last faint glow of the sunset, the ship was raising sail. LeBoux had given up trying to find them and left them for dead.

Chapter 17
Rising Storm

The wind was getting stronger and the seas were up. Clouds were gathering, blotting out the stars. Darkness was nearly total.

Jack had managed to refill the leather air bag before the sea had come to its full fury. The storm was stirring up huge swells and pounding waves, the wind had risen nearly into a gale. There was nothing that Jack or his two floundering companions could do but hang on. They had wrapped the air bag's ropes tightly around their wrists, knowing it was their only chance. Still it wasn't going well. They were being tossed around and into each other. Violent waves would come thundering down upon them. Then they would be sucked down below the surface by the swirling current, only to come up and be pounded again.

There were only two things in their favor. They weren't a long way from shore and the wind was blowing them right for it.

Soon Jack could see the occasional lights ashore. They were being carried along west-southwest and the shoreline was getting closer. As they approached landfall, Jack knew they had one more concern. But that, like the rest of their time adrift, was largely beyond their control. If they came ashore at a cliff or onto rocks, they would be in serious trouble. There were a lot of beaches along the coast, he wondered if they would be lucky enough to end up on one.

Although the past hour or so riding out the stormy sea had done its best to wear him down, Jack's senses were alert. He could see a few flickering lights a little to the south, but they weren't heading that way. They were being carried straight toward land and darkness. Jack could hear loud sounds toward shore and he recognized those sounds. It was clearly waves crashing against rocks. He instantly began kicking south, in the direction of the lights he had seen. He then realized that the leather bag was only slowing them down, preventing him from using both arms. He called out to Fawn and Dan, "We've got to get clear of the rocks! Let go of the bag and grab onto my clothes, we've got to swim for it!"

In spite of the force of the waves, Fawn and Dan did manage to cling to either side of his shirt. Jack began using his powerful arms and legs to try and clear the rocks. He was swimming fast and hard, using every bit of what strength he had left. It was a desperate and frantic effort with the sound of the sea against the rocks just to their right. Then, with exhaustion draining Jack's wind and body, another wave struck. A wall of water came thundering over them, and they were sucked down into dark current. They came up coughing and gasping for air. Jack's effort had been enough though, for the crashing sounds were then just behind them.

Another strong wave picked all three up and threw them hard onto the shore. They came rolling up a fairly steep gravel-strewn beach, only to get hit again by one more strong wave as they lay choking, coughing, and trying to catch their breath. Not surprisingly, his companions had been of little help in the last swimming effort. They were exhausted. It was also up to Jack to pull them the rest of the way up the beach beyond the surf.

From the effort, Jack dropped to the moist, pebble-covered beach beside Fawn and Dan. All three laid there in a state of exhaustion for a long while. They found themselves huddling together against the cold wind just beyond the surf, with the jungle not far behind them. There were few words spoken; they were that tired. They needed time to catch their breath and gather their strength.

Soon lightning began piercing the dark sky. With the flashes of light, Jack could see just how close they had come to the rocks. A little to his left was a natural, jettylike wall of rock that angled out to sea. They had barely missed it coming in. It was useful for the moment because it was blocking some of the wind. He stood up, waited for the next lightning flash, and looked north, over the wall of rock. There was a rugged line of rock that met the sea and a scattering of various-sized rocks protruding out of the water. That was no place to come ashore. It had been a close call.

Jack offered Fawn and Dan a hand and got them to their feet. He nudged them along the twenty odd steps over to the jetty wall. They sat down with their backs against the rocks and Fawn in the middle. It was better there. The cold wind was mostly deflected over them by the wall of rocks.

Jack put his arms around her and held her tight. He felt her shivering and breathing fast. Dan was breathing a little hard too. Jack tended to recover from exertion pretty fast. He was wet and cold, just as they were, but otherwise he was feeling better. He waited a few minutes to let them catch their breath and then asked, "So, how are you two doing?"

Fawn's voice was a little labored and quivered from being cold. "I'll be alright once I get warm."

"What about you, Dan?"

"I'm mighty cold, and I must have drank ten gallons of salt water. But mostly I'm madder than a wet hen."

"The pirates." Jack knew what he meant.

"Remember the first time we saw those scallywags in that restaurant?"

"Yeah."

"We should've let you thump 'em, like you wanted to."

Fawn turned around toward Dan. "What good would that have done?"

"It'd make me feel a heck of a lot better right now! Why, those dirty pirates took the gold, our guns, heck, everything." He shook his head. "Got away scot-free too."

"I don't think so," Jack stated flatly. "LeBoux wouldn't stay at sea in this storm. He would've headed straight for shelter at the port. He'll wait out the storm in Vera Cruz before going on. And if he's still there when we get back, I'll get our guns back."

Fawn pulled back from Jack a little, her voice went sharp. "We no sooner escape with our lives, and you're planning to take on those pirates!"

"That's not exactly true. It's pretty much been on my mind ever since I saw them leveling all those rifles at me. It just wasn't the right time yet."

Fawn wasn't good at staying mad at him for very long. After a moment or two she dropped her head and fell into his arms once again. They stayed there a while longer, watching the lightning move closer.

Jack knew they couldn't stay where they were. They were already chilled to the bone and the rains were coming. He helped his companions to their feet and urged them on. The lights he saw were a little to the south. If they followed the edge of the jungle in that direction, they would find shelter.

In the darkness, it was tricky going. They could barely see what was right in front of them. It was a matter of feeling their way along. A clumsy, groping process. The sporadic lightning helped a little, but most of the venture was tediously slow. Being barefoot, Jack's feet took a beating. Another reason to hate LeBoux, but he didn't need another reason.

After about a half hour, they came to the source of the lights. It was a fish camp built way back on a long beach. Lights still flickered from behind the small windows of the four makeshift wood and palm frond shacks. A bolt of lightning out to sea momentarily illuminated the beach. A half-dozen fishing boats and accompanying nets were resting midway up the white sand beach.

Jack led the way to the nearest hut. It was a crudely constructed dwelling, made of various sized and shaped wooden poles and covered with palm leaves. The odor of fish was predominant. As they approached, there was also the smell of beans and tortillas from within. They had arrived at dinner time. It was a delicious aroma, although they didn't really need to be reminded of just how hungry they were.

From Jack's experience with Mexican people, especially the rural folk, he was not surprised that they were welcomed inside and offered to share their food. In fact, it was generally true that a Mexican family would give up their own food and bed for a stranger, even if it meant they might go hungry. They were that hospitable.

An older husband and wife, Carlos and Elda, shared the smallish quarters. The three extra guests made things pretty tight, but no one seemed to mind. The couple were warm and generous, and the guests were grateful. They were given heavy blankets to wrap themselves in and their clothes were hung by the iron stove to dry. Dinner was served as the rains arrived. Fried fish with beans and tortillas was the night's meal. The fish was good. As hungry as they were, it hardly mattered.

With dinner over, they found a place near the stove to bed down. The wind howled and the rain pelted against the palapa roof. Jack was relieved that Fawn and Dan had come through their ordeal at sea unscathed. He watched them sleeping soundly for a while and found himself smiling fondly at Fawn's sweet face. Finally, he lay his head back and closed his eyes. He slept uneasily though, waking often with LeBoux and his men on his mind.

They awoke early to the sounds of rattling pots and pans. Señora Elda was getting the morning meal underway. Breakfast would be little different from supper. The fish was garnished with butter instead of tomato sauce.

The wind, rain, and heavy seas had not diminished. There would be no fishing on such a day.

Their clothes were dry by then, and they got dressed quickly. Dan had a few dollars tucked into his pants pockets. It took some coaxing, but they managed to convince Señor Carlos to take the money. In return, he offered to take them back to Vera Cruz.

After breakfast they were each given a length of canvas to fend off the weather. Then after the three guests thanked Elda for her considerable hospitality, Carlos led them a little ways into the jungle to a corral. There were two carts residing alongside the corral, two wet and unhappy-looking burros stood inside. They hitched up a burro to each of the carts and headed south.

Dan rode in the lead cart with their Mexican friend. Jack and Fawn followed close behind in the second one. It was a rough and pitching ride. The two wheeled carts had no springs, no seat, and reeked of decaying fish. They knelt inside the box-like wagon and did their best to stay covered up. It was an unpleasant journey.

The trip into Vera Cruz, other than the weather, was a routine event for Carlos. Taking the rugged and wandering road through the jungle was how the fishermen brought their catch to market.

The rain and wind continued and the muddy conditions had slowed their progress. It was late morning when they entered the city. They came in along the docks. The weather had not deterred commerce. As they passed a ship from the Orient, they noticed the dockworkers were busily unloading giant looms of silk. Fawn seemed fascinated with the assorted shipping businesses. There were fitters that made everything from sail and rigging to masts and timbers. Farther along they went by less nautical commerce, household items like metal stoves and wicker furniture. Jack noticed that even those rather ordinary shops caught her eye. He enjoyed her endless curiosity. She was shivering from the cold, but her sharp mind and spirit was undampened.

They were soon nearing their hotel. Just as they made the turn that led to the Hotel Serenidad, Jack strained his eyes through the gray mist toward the docks ahead. There, just about where it was before, was the dark shape of the *Azteca*. As he pondered how he could overcome such poor odds, they arrived at the hotel. Jack jumped out to help Fawn down from the wagon to the street. He then quickly tied the reins of the second burro to the lead cart before joining Dan and Carlos. They all thanked their most gracious amigo, shook his hand, and bid him adios. With one snap of the reins, he continued up the cobbled street with the second cart in tow.

They then ducked into the hotel lobby and out of the weather. Behind the counter was Javier, but he was not wearing his usual smile. In fact, he wore a most troubled expression. He swallowed once before he spoke in an aggetated tone. "Señor McCall, they're coming for you!"

"Who is?" Jack asked casually, as he pulled the soaked canvas from over his head and shoulders.

"The *federales*. The Mexican army!"

Chapter 18
Lying Low

J avier quickly rounded the counter, went to the door, and looked in both directions. Satisfied that no one was outside to see who had just entered his hotel, he turned back to Jack. "Follow me, *rapido!*"

He led them down the hallway in the opposite direction of the old room to the very last door, opened it, and motioned them in. After following them inside, he closed the door behind him and turned to Jack, Fawn, and Dan, all standing to his right. "Señor Jack, the *policia* came around this morning to look at the hotel registry. They do that once or twice a week. Anyway, when they saw your name they asked about you, and I told them."

"What, exactly, did you tell them?" Jack felt he had to interrupt at that point.

"I told them about the show I saw you in. And what you could do with guns." He paused to swallow. His words then seemed to come with reluctance. "But then they said you were wanted for murder. That you gunned down two unarmed men in Nogales." He looked hard at Jack and his eyes narrowed. "This cannot be true."

Jack just shook his head.

"I knew there was some mistake, and I told them so. I told them you wouldn't do such a thing. You wouldn't have to. No two men would have a chance against you."

"What else did they say?"

"They said that you were too dangerous. They would come back tomorrow with the army."

"Why tomorrow?"

"The *federales* are out on patrol. They're not supposed to be back until then.

Jack looked to the solemn faces to his right. Dan spoke up first. "I know you're good partner, but I don't think you want to take on the Mexican army, even if you had your guns."

Jack gave a half smile as Javier glanced down at Jack's waist.

"Where are your guns, Señor Jack?"

"It's a long story, but I figure on getting them back tonight."

Javier seemed puzzled by his answer, but returned, "You can stay here for now. It's not safe in the street— the *policia* know you're in Vera Cruz. I wouldn't leave until dark."

Jack put his right hand on Javier's shoulder. "I know you're sticking your neck out for me. *Gracias, amigo.*"

He shook his head. "*Por nada, amigo.*" He then turned and left the room.

Jack turned to Fawn. For a few moments, he tried to soothe her tense expression with a smile. He then took her in his arms and held her tight. During the embrace he remembered the necklace in his pocket.

He had wanted to wait until the right moment to give her what he had found in the temple. *There would be no better time,* he thought. He whispered in her ear, "I have a little present for you."

She moved her head back in surprise. "A present?"

He reached into his pocket, pulled out the green-colored golden object, and put it into her hands. "It needs some cleaning, but I hope this will do."

She seemed stunned, looking down at the heavy chain and medallion and back up to Jack's face. Then, without uttering a word, she rushed over to the vanity. A pitcher of water, basin, soap, and towels had been provided atop the small table. A small square mirror rested around eye level on the wall behind the table. After pouring water into the basin, she briefly immersed the necklace in the water and started scrubbing. She would hold a section in her hand and then lather up the pumice soap over the chain in her hand. Then she'd use her fingers in and around the intricate gold artifact. After a minute, or so, Jack and Dan went to the nearest bed and sat down. It would, apparently, take a while for the cleaning.

The room was very much like the previous one. Three beds in a row, the vanity table, and not much else. Jack did notice that Javier had placed Dan and his bedrolls between the first two beds. Fawn's bedroll was at the foot of the last one.

The minutes dragged on. After what was close to a half hour, she dried the necklace with a towel and presented it to Jack for inspection. Her face was beaming. Jack returned a smile of satisfaction. Dan craned over to study the glistening object held in Jack's lap. The chain was made of simple round links of heavy gold. The medallion was also of gold. It was smooth and flat on one side. The other side was encrusted with emeralds. A large jewel was in the very center. Smaller stones circled the outer edge of the disk.

As Jack and Dan momentarily sat there admiring the beauty of the piece, Fawn seemed to be growing anxious. She turned away and began slowly pacing around the room. Jack looked up from the necklace and watched her move about the room. She was in deep thought and didn't even notice his eyes following her. Briefly, she paused to glance at her bedroll. She then made her way back to Jack and Dan and stopped. There was a look of resolve on her face. Then her expression softened, giving Jack a warm smile. "Let's see how it looks on me."

He stood up, slipped the gold necklace over her head, lifted her long hair through the chain and let it fall. The medallion was over three inches across. The long chain placed it midway to her waist. It was quite beautiful, but rather large for her petite frame. His eyes went from the medallion to her eyes. "I didn't realize it was so big."

She went to the mirror and posed before it for a few seconds. Then she returned to Jack, giving him a terse nod and smiling, "Well, I love it!"

"That's all that counts." He put his left hand beneath her chin, lifted it slightly, and kissed her. After a moment or two, she hugged him and then stepped back. "All right, like Javier said, it's not safe for you to leave here during daylight. So Dan and I are going to be gone for a while." Her eyes narrowed a little. "You wait here!"

"Where are you going?"

"It won't be easy to get you out of here with the Mexican police and army after you, but I've got an idea."

"So what is it?"

She moved close to him and looked sincerely into his eyes. "Do you trust me?"

"Of course."

"Well, this time you'll have to do just that."

Jack could only watch as she went to her bedroll, pulled out the science magazine, and motioned for Dan to follow. As she walked toward the door, she concealed the very conspicuous necklace by slipping it behind the bodice of her white cotton dress. Dan was now standing. He looked to Jack, who simply shrugged. Dan gave another shrug in return before heading for the door. As they left, Jack stated, "Be careful," and the door closed behind them.

There was nothing for him to do but lay low, while wondering what she was up to.

Before she and Dan left the hotel, they stopped at the desk. Javier greeted them with a smile. "Anything I can help with?"

Fawn nodded. "Is there a rich person in this town interested in Aztec treasure?"

"What do you mean by treasure, señorita?"

She glanced around, making sure there were no eyes nearby and then pulled the necklace out from within her dress. "Like this."

He had a startled look. "*Aye Chihuahua! Muy bonita.* It's beautiful, señorita." He put his hand beneath the medallion and looked closer. Then he lifted it slightly, judging its weight. "You must see Señor Madera, Juan Miguel Madera."

"Would he be interested in this?"

"Oh, yes. He has many ancient pieces. He collects them. Señor Madera is the man you must see."

"Where can I find him?"

"He has several businesses along the docks. He could be at any of them. Just go along the wharf toward the shipping business. When you see the name Madera, go in and ask. They should be able to tell you where he is."

"*Gracias*, Javier." She slipped the necklace back inside her dress and headed for the door. Dan gave a grateful nod to their Mexican friend as he followed her outside.

As the door closed behind them, he put his hand on her shoulder, causing her to turn toward him. "Are you going to tell me what we're doing and why you're selling that medallion?"

"If I tell you, you'll tell me I'm crazy. I don't want to be talked out of this, Dan. I think it's our best chance of keeping Jack out of jail or worse. Just give me some time to see if my idea could really work."

Dan gave a little shrug. "Alright, you're the thinker around here. But I'd sure feel better knowin' how you're gonna do it."

"I'm not so sure you would," she stated as she turned and headed for the docks.

The rain had eased to a drizzle while the wind still blew steadily off the sea. They made their way back along the docks in the direction they had come in that morning. Few people had been out in the hostile weather, except in the commercial district, where it was business as usual. Soon, they came to the first enterprise owned by Señor Madera. It was called Equipales De Madera, a maker of wicker furniture. The workers inside the small shop suggested that their boss would likely be found at his warehouse. It was about midway up the dock fronts.

The name *Bodega Madera* was prominent above the bay doors of the huge wooden building. Its white paint was both faded and peeling. Not surprising since it received a regular battering from the wind and rain, also exposure to damp salt air. A worker directed them to his office at the far right corner of the warehouse.

The door was open. Fawn stood in the doorway for a moment before the middle-aged and rather distinguished-looking gentleman stood up from behind his oak desk and motioned them in. As they stood before him, Señor Madera broke the silence with, "How may I serve you?" His voice was soft and pleasant, and he spoke surprisingly good English. His manner was polite.

Fawn's Spanish was not so practiced as the man's English and she was happy that she wouldn't have to rely on it. "I understand you have an interest in Aztec jewelry."

His face answered before he spoke. "Yes. It's true. I collect Aztec art. I'm interested in their pottery, sculpture, and especially jewelry. What do you have?"

She pulled the necklace over her head and handed it to him. He seemed entranced, carefully examining it for nearly a minute without saying a word. He finally pulled his attention from the piece and shook his head.

"It is amazing—two rare treasures of the Aztecs in the same day!"

"What do you mean, two pieces?"

"Why, just this morning, two men brought another piece of Aztec gold here. They also wanted to sell it."

"A large disk? A golden sun?" She couldn't hide her displeasure and glanced toward Dan. He had a similar expression.

"You know these men?"

"Captain LeBoux and his first mate?"

He nodded.

"Our paths have crossed, but I wouldn't want them to know you've seen us."

"Of course, señorita. But I have no reason to see them again. Le Boux wanted far more money than I could give them."

"More than it's worth?"

"I don't think so. But I told him it was more than anyone around here could pay. He will probably have no trouble selling it in the United States, but I think it belongs here. It's a part of our history."

She gave a couple nods. "So are you interested in the necklace?"

"Yes, but what do you want for it?"

She had the science magazine rolled up and was holding it in her right hand. Using both hands, she pulled it flat and flipped through a few pages. She then turned it toward Señor Madera and placed it on his desk before him. "This is what I want." She put her finger on the page. "I've read about this and given it a lot of thought. I know it's possible."

For a few moments, he simply stared at the page with

great concentration. Finally, he looked up with something of a satisfied smile. "We have everything to do this at the businesses along the dock."

Fawn returned the smile. "I know. So what do you say?"

"Is this all you want . . . nothing else?"

"Well, one thing." Her face was dead serious. "I want it today."

"Today!" He almost shouted it. His eyes went very wide.

"Tonight at the latest."

He sat back in his chair. His eyes seemed to go all around the small office and finally down. Soon he closed his eyes as the matter consumed his thoughts. After a very long moment, he looked up at Fawn and gave a single nod. "I think we can do this, but it will be close. I will send for more workers and put as many people on it as needed. All other work in my businesses will stop until it is finished. But you must stay and help oversee this. You and I must show them what to do."

She smiled. "Of course."

Dan had managed to stay out of their negotiations, but at that point, his curiosity drove him to take a peek. He stepped up to the desk, reached for the magazine, and turned it toward him. His head then snapped back from the shock. With a blank expression, he turned to Fawn. "This is your idea?"

She answered with a couple nods.

He tried to swallow, but found it difficult.

Chapter 19
A Score To Settle

Jack had spent a restless day within the hotel room. Being cooped up in his small, stark quarters had made him edgy. He had plenty on his mind. The Mexican police and army wanted him, and he didn't even have a gun. Later that night, he would have go after LeBoux with little more than his wits. And then there was Fawn. It wasn't like her to be so secretive.

There was little for him to do until dark. He had removed the short ropes used to tie the bedrolls and tied them end to end. That gave him about a ten-foot length of rope, which he made into a lasso. Other than that and his knife, he had no weapons. Even so, Jack figured he had a fair chance. LeBoux most certainly believed him to be dead. The captain's guard would likely be down. The fact that Jack knew his way around the ship would also help. Surprise and darkness, however, were his best allies. But it was a long time until sundown. He would simply have to wait. He lay down on the first bed and tried to get some rest. The hours ticked slowly by.

The room finally began to grow a little darker. A shadowy hue signaled the end of the day. Jack then heard footsteps coming down the hallway, making him alert. He sat up on the bed just as he heard three rapid knocks on the door. It opened and Dan walked casually in. "How you doin', partner?"

"Nevermind me. What's going on out there?"

"Well, the wind's still blowin' but the rain stopped."

"I don't mean that! What about Fawn?" It wasn't like Jack to be terse with Dan.

"That's why I'm here. It's gonna be dark pretty soon. She wants you ready to go in about an hour. She also hoped you changed your mind about goin' after LeBoux, but didn't think there was much chance of that."

Jack shook his head. "So, what's she up to?"

"She thinks you've got enough on your mind without knowin' about it. I think she's right."

He just twisted his mouth.

"And you were right about LeBoux. The ship's still there. I could just see it as I made the corner coming here, but I didn't want to go any closer."

He nodded.

"And don't ask me how I know, but it looks like he's still got the golden sun."

"Anything else I'm not supposed to know about?"

"Sorry it has to be like this, partner, but it's for the best. You just do what you have to do, then make your way down toward the warehouses."

"What will I look for?"

Dan smiled. "I don't think you'll have trouble finding us." He reached back for the door and added, "I asked our friend Javier to stroll on by the *Azteca* and take a look-see. Might be nice to know what you're goin' up against."

Jack returned another nod. "Thanks, Dakota, but what's your hurry?"

"Got work to do," he stated with a smile and left.

An hour was not a lot of time for what Jack had to do. He grabbed the rope, coiled it up, and paced the room. About ten minutes passed before he heard more footsteps coming his way. He figured that he knew who it was and didn't wait. Jack met Javier halfway down the hallway. "You've been by the ship, *amigo?*"

"*Si*, your friend explained things to me, so I went down and did a little spying. I walked by real slow. Now, I only saw one man on deck, but I heard voices in the captain's cabin. On the way back I stopped at the cantina on the other side of the street. I know the owner and thought I'd see if he'd heard anything. He told me that most sailors thought the storm was almost over. He also said that he'd overheard one from the *Azteca* say they were sailing tomorrow."

"*Gracias*, I owe you for all you've done."

"No, my friend, it's been an honor to be of service to you."

Jack then gave his amigo a firm handshake, made his way out of the hotel, and headed for the docks.

It was nearly dark by then. The wind was cool but not nearly so strong. The damp cobbled street felt cold against his bare feet. He got to the end of the street and looked around. There were few people out and about. He looked down along the dock toward the *Azteca*. He could make out the yellow glow of the two rear windows of the captain's cabin.

He had no reason to delay. Javier saw only one man on deck. There was no way of knowing when the crew might start coming back from shore leave. Jack went to the dockside, looked around one more time, and slipped into the water. He put the rope around his neck and then began quietly swimming for the ship. It took only a few minutes to reach the stern of the black schooner.

He paused there momentarily to look and listen. All he could hear was the ship's hull rubbing against it's moorings. He briefly considered climbing to the deck there, but then noted the anchor up forward.

Silently he moved ahead until he was right under the anchor. Because the ship was tied to the dock, the anchor had not been dropped. It hung suspended by it's chain just below the deck, parallel to the hull. He pulled the rope over his head and unwound it. It took him one try to put the lasso around the anchor's right fluke. Then he pulled himself up the rope, hand over hand, until he reached the iron anchor that had been no more than six foot above the water. It was still several more feet up to the deck. At that point it was a matter of grabbing hold of the anchor itself to pull himself up. When he reached the chain, he was able to put his left leg over the left fluke and slip his rope free. After recoiling the rope and putting it back around his neck, he continued the ascent. Within seconds, he was at eye level with the deck.

It was important to know how many were topside. He

was able to place both of his feet atop the anchor flukes and give his hands and arms a rest as he watched. A full minute passed by as Jack studied the single swabby as he slowly strolled the deck. He was a fairly large man, dressed in a blue-and-white striped shirt topped with a solid blue cap.

Convinced that he had just one man to deal with, Jack began his plan. He dropped down a little ways on the anchor chain and then pulled his feet above his head, but in a crouch. He was hanging upside down with his knees to his chest and his feet just below the deck.

Bird sounds were not a particular talent of Jack's, but he could do a decent dove call. He began making the cooing sound while listening for the seaman's approach. After a little time, footsteps grew closer on the creaking deck. Jack's body tensed like a tightly wound spring as the footsteps stopped just above him. Because of the darkness and the way the deck extended slightly beyond the bow, neither man could see the other. Jack made one more coo and could hear the sailor moving. He did as Jack figured. Curiousity made him kneel down to peer over the side. As he did, Jack kicked straight up with his right foot, just as hard as he could. It caught the man under the chin and he fell, out cold.

Jack dropped his feet back down and then pulled himself back to eye level with the deck. It hadn't been much of a fight and not very loud. Just the thud of Jack's foot against the man's chin and him falling backward onto his back. For a few seconds he paused and waited to see if it had drawn anyone's attention from within LeBoux's cabin. It wasn't surprising that such sounds would be ignored. There were always a certain amount of noises aboard a ship. Ropes and furled sail would rustle against the wind. The ship itself creaked and rocked back and forth against its moorings.

Jack lifted a leg over and eased himself quietly onto the deck. He took a quick look at the unconscious sailor and knew he would be out for quite a while. At that moment he also noticed a bulge beneath the man's shirt. He had a small caliber pistol tucked inside his waist. His shirttail had concealed it. *That figured*, Jack thought. If you've got a ship filled with illegal guns, you don't want to draw attention to yourself. And merchant sailors don't usually carry guns. He liberated the weapon from him and removed a couple of other things, too. *A little disguise couldn't hurt*, Jack mused. He slipped the man's shirt and cap on and then headed for the hold.

The ladder leading below deck was adjacent to the captain's quarters. Jack went a few steps down, so he was nearly out of sight, and just listened for a few seconds. He wasn't particularly interested in what they were saying, just who was inside. Once he was satisfied that it was only LeBoux and his first mate, he continued down into the ship's hold.

A single lantern hung on an overhead beam. Its wick had been turned down so it barely glowed. Jack took hold of it, turned up the wick, and gave the the ship's belly a careful inspection. Of course it was the golden sun that he wanted. He didn't really expect to find it so far from LeBoux's grasp, but he had to be sure.

The ship's cargo was stacked from where Jack stood,

all the way forward. It was lashed down with ropes and cargo nets, with a small walking space left on each side. High above each of the walking spaces, strung to overhead beams, were a half-dozen hammocks. Behind him in the area that lay directly below the captain's quarters was the crew's mess. Three rugged-looking tables and accompanying chairs stood midway in that space. Behind that, stacked up all the way astern, were the ship's provisions. To Jack's right, assorted tools, mops, and buckets lay in disarray by the port-side wall.

Jack carried the lantern up foward for a closer look. The first of the cargo was innocent looking enough. Simply barrels of flour, rice, and wheat. Way up in the bow, however, and draped with canvas to conceal it were the guns. He pulled back the canvas to find enough rifle crates and cases of cartridges to start a small war.

As he figured, the sun was not there. It seemed to him that it might take a little extra persuasion to get the captain to tell him where it was. So Jack made his way back toward the ship's stern. Along the way he pulled off a blanket from one of the hammocks and headed for the tools. He pushed the blanket down into a metal bucket, removed the reservoir cap from the lantern, and poured the remainder of its kerosene over the blanket. The center table was right under LeBoux's floor. Jack put the pail on that table, removed the lantern's globe, and touched the flame to the fuel-soaked cloth. The smoky flame rose about a foot, but Jack knew it would soon smolder. It was the smoke that he was after.

With his plan set in motion, he climbed the ladder, noting that no one else had come back to the ship, and got ready to surprise LeBoux. He pulled the cap down over his eyes, held the pistol behind his back, and entered LeBoux's quarters with his head held low. At first they hardly paid attention to the man who just entered the room. As Jack lifted his head and they saw who it was, they both dropped their cards and stared in disbelief. Billy seemed frozen in fear. LeBoux was also scared, but Jack sensed that there was still some fight left in him.

Having gotten the drop on his two enemies, Jack stood up straight and let the pistol hang to his side. He took in the cabin's interior with a single glance. The captain and his first mate had been playing poker at a small table two steps before him. The two men sat across from each other, LeBoux was to his right. Behind them and spanning half the width of the room was a bunk. A sea chest resided at both ends of the bed. On the right-hand wall was a desk with tools, charts, and other aids for navigation. Against the opposing wall was a chest of drawers. What interested Jack most was one of his own pistols. It was lying on the far side of the card table and the captain's right hand was cautiously moving toward it. Another thing he noticed was the expressions on the two men. All color seemed to be drained from their faces. They wore a look of considerable shock.

Jack looked into the men's frightened faces. "You two look like you just saw death show up at your door." Jack glanced down at the cards laying on the table, then back to the men. "Sorry to interrupt the game, boys, but your luck just ran out."

Billy's eyes were wide and he seemed to be paralyzed. LeBoux, while still inching his hand for the gun, swallowed hard and managed, "You're a hard man to kill."

"I never found killing very hard. Just keep moving your hand for that gun, and I'll show you how easy it is."

As LeBoux's hand retreated back away from the pistol, Jack looked to the first mate. "I'd like my gun back. Hand it to me, by the barrel." Billy was the more nervous of the two and less likely to try something. Jack didn't want to kill anybody. At least not until he got what he came for.

With a trembling hand, Billy reached across the table and made the handoff. Jack then pointed one pistol at each man. "All right. One way or another, I'm taking what you stole from me." Jack clicked the hammers back on both guns to make the point. "You better tell me where it is if you plan on living."

LeBoux looked Jack over, his eyes narrowed some. "You won't kill us in cold blood. You're not the sort."

"And you're willing to bet your life on that." Jack raised his eyebrows a bit. "Come to think of it, you just did."

Of course the captain was right, but he couldn't read that from Jack's hard stare and cool manner. LeBoux could see Jack's hands and expression tighten and the captain started to sweat. He finally gave in. "Alright, your things are in that chest at the foot of the bed." LeBoux gave that information grudgingly. Jack knew he was stalling.

By that time the scent of smoke was in the air. Because the cabin was not well lit, it was barely visible. But as it continued to seep through the cracks in the floor, that would soon change.

Jack went to the chest while keeping an eye on the seamen. He knelt beside it, opened the lid, and took the minute or so it took to put on his duds and gunbelt. He also noted that his money was no longer inside his boot. After throwing Dan's holster over his left shoulder, he went back to his enemies.

By that time, the smoke had gotten thick enough to burn their eyes and Jack could see that they had something else to wonder about. Before Jack could speak, LeBoux blurted out, "Where's that smoke coming from?"

"I'll get to that in a minute. First, I want the golden sun."

"It's not here."

"You wouldn't let it be very far from you. Now you better tell me quick because it's going to start getting hot in here. I started a fire down in the hold."

"Are you crazy! There's ammunition down there. This thing's going to blow up!"

Jack gave him a doubtful expression. "You expect me to believe that? No one's leaving until I get that sun." It wasn't going to be long before one of the men lost their nerve. He could see it in their eyes.

Up until that point, Billy had remained mute, letting his captain do the talking. But he finally had enough. He motioned with his head toward the bed, "It's under the bunk! Now let us out of here!"

Jack kept his right pistol aimed at the two men as he went to retrieve the golden disk. It had been wrapped in a thick blanket. He quickly got hold of it, lifted a corner to see the gleaming gold finish, and then tucked the heavy object under his left arm.

He went back to the pirates. Even the captain seemed relieved that the cat-and-mouse game was over. He was only interested in survival by then. Jack motioned for them to stand with his revolver and then ushered them out the door. Smoke was spewing from the hold, causing additional panic to the seamen's nerves. They started to bolt for the gangway, but Jack stopped them short. "Hold it, boys! Not that way." He directed them toward the port side of the ship and walked up behind them. They were looking back over their shoulders at him, their faces tense with terror. "If there's really ammunition below, you'd better get as far from this ship as you can. But you're not following me. You're going that way." He pointed out into the bay. "One more thing. You stole some money from me. I'll take whatever you have on you." They both scrambled into their pockets and passed the bills back to him. Then as they turned to dive, Jack gave them each a hard shove. They splashed ungainly into the water and he turned back for the dock. It had taken a while to deal with the scoundrels. He hoped not too long. Fawn and Dan were waiting for him, but that was all he knew.

Chapter 20
High Risk Plan

Time was not on Jack's side. Still he wanted to make sure that LeBoux's deadly cargo went no farther. As he headed back to meet Dan and Fawn, he decided to make a little detour and tell Javier about the guns. He figured that his amigo could go to the policia since he could not.

When he came to the street of the hotel, he rounded the corner, but stopped short. Up the cobbled street and right in front of the hotel were gathered dozens of soldiers. In the moment that he stood there motionless, two of them turned his way. There was the briefest of time where they simply eyed one another. Trying not to bring any more attention to himself, Jack slowly turned back and continued across the street in the direction of the warehouses. Once he was out of their sight, he broke into a dead run.

He hadn't seen an officer among the troops. The man in command was probably inside the hotel. One of the soldiers that saw him would have to go in and report what he had seen. Jack hoped the army would take some time to get organized. He continued to run, but the heavy and awkward disk slowed his progress. A glance over his shoulder determined that no one was yet in pursuit, but he knew they'd be coming.

Jack passed by a series of stores and shops along the dock. None of that was even noticed by him. His eyes were fixed on the light, noises, and image ahead. In the boatyard, next to the sailmaker's shop, was a flurry of activity, lights, and people.

An iron fence surrounded the large square lot used for fitting and repairing all types of boats. It was a dry dock with a metal and carpentry shop on the far right. A little nearer and toward the center, was a large brick forge, normally used for metal work. Ordinarily, the forge and the yard would be used for sundry boat work, but not that night. All the boats, jigs, timbers, and other tools and equipment had been moved all the way back against the rear wall to make room for something else.

Jack passed through the long open gate and approached the crowd. He was a little winded and obviously concerned about the army, but for a few seconds, he simply stopped and stared at a most unexpected sight. As Dan and Fawn spotted him and rushed up to him, he just stood there, watching the huge hot-air balloon sway back and forth in the wind.

In those few moments, as Jack took in the multicolored silk sphere with the wicker passenger basket beneath attached by ropes, Señor Madera joined them. Jack managed to break his attention away from the balloon and saw Dan and Fawn, who were then at his side. He turned to Fawn, "I think the army's right behind me!"

Señor Madera spoke up from just behind. "Señor, permit me. I think I can delay the *federales*."

Jack didn't waste time with a single word. He just motioned in the direction from which they were coming.

Madera went to the crowd with a raised right hand and spoke to them in Spanish so fast that neither Jack nor Fawn understood much of it. But with that rapid little speech, the whole of the crowd swarmed back to meet the army.

In the time it took for Señor Madera to convey his directions to his workers, Fawn showed Jack the article about the development of balloons in France. Because of the circumstances, he gave it but a glance. If he'd had time to read it, he would have found it interesting. Besides telling the history of lighter-than-air craft, it illustrated design and construction plans. It also included the formula for size and load calculations.

She then explained that Señor Madera had commandeered every seamstress and sailmaker in Vera Cruz for the project. He also had most of the shops along the docks involved too. Of course, Jack knew how she had paid for it. Rather than mention it, he simply lifted her chin and kissed her.

Jack then glanced down at the base of the wicker basket and saw that there were four ropes tied to large stakes in the ground, tethering the balloon. In addition, he noticed how the forge had been altered to fill the balloon. They had made a makeshift, *S*-shaped funnel that went from the furnace chimney over and up into the

opening below the balloon. Three men were still kneeling at the furnace, working the bellows.

Jack and company knew the delaying tactic wouldn't hold the army for long and headed for the balloon. On the way Jack had to ask, "Is this thing done? Is it ready to go?"

Fawn nodded. "Yeah, they finished putting the last of the varnish on the silk about an hour ago."

"So why were they all still here?"

She smiled. "I think they wanted to see if it would really fly."

Jack nodded. "I was kind of wondering the same thing."

Dan was just to his partner's left and spoke up to Jack's ear. "I gotta admit that's been on my mind the whole dang day."

Señor Madera rejoined them next to the basket. "It is time, my friends." He pulled out a small knife from his belt. "I will cut the lines when you're ready." He then looked at the blanket-covered object under Jack's arm. "May I see it, please?"

Jack glanced back to see if he could see the army. Voices could be heard from that way, but that was all. He withdrew the heavy golden disk from the blanket and handed it to him. It was the first time Jack had really seen it. The green algae had been polished off and the intricate detail of engraved flames were visible in gleaming gold.

As Madera held the ancient relic and marveled at its beauty, Fawn whispered into Jack's ear. "Let him have it, sweetheart. It should stay in Mexico."

He smiled and gave her a single nod. "I was thinking the same thing." He gave another look at the balloon. "Besides, I don't think we need any extra weight."

He then offered her a hand and helped her into the basket. Dan went around to the other side and climbed in too. Jack entered next to Fawn and turned back to Señor Madera. "We won't be taking that along. It belongs here."

Señor Madera seemed suddenly choked for words. He turned and motioned for the men on the bellows to remove the tin pipes providing the hot air and stepped closer to the basket. "You have let us keep our history." He reached into his pocket and retrieved a large roll of bills. "This is not enough for what you've done, but please, take it."

Jack knew the money would be useful for the trip home. He also didn't want to waste any more time. He accepted it with, "*Gracias.*"

Madera then looked to Fawn. "Now, before I cut the lines, you must light the furnace." He handed her a box of matches.

Jack inspected the rectangular metal device with its round stovepipe pointing into the opening of the balloon. He watched her turn a valve, open a small sliding door at the base of the furnace, and then reach in and light it. It lit with a loud whoosh, and she closed the door. As she began adjusting the flame, she gave the signal to cut the lines.

The three men who had been manning the brick furnace went to the basket to help steady it as Madera went around to cut the tether ropes. The breeze was still blowing steady from the sea and was causing the balloon to lean and sway as it pulled against the ropes. As

Madera cut the last rope, he held on to it while the three men allowed the basket to raise above their heads. At that point, the balloon started pulling them along and they all let go.

With a suddenness, the balloon went up and across the yard. It picked up speed fast. As it barely cleared the yard's equipment and rear wall, they looked down and back toward the crowd. Some of the soldiers had just made their way past the swarm of people and were entering the boatyard. It hadn't been desperately close, but close enough.

At that point the basket was skirting across the rooftops while still gaining speed. There was a half-moon raising just above the mountains to the west. It appeared between the last remaining clouds, casting a welcome glow against the night sky. Slowly the balloon rose higher and the people around the boatyard became ever smaller and farther behind. Jack gave a quick survey in all directions. He could see the many lights below that illuminated Vera Cruz. Beyond the city were only the occasional dots of light that indicated a home or small village. To the west was the dark silhouette of the mountains.

Between them and the mountains was jungle. Jack knew that was no place to try and come down. What awaited them at or beyond the mountains was unknown to him. They were continuing to gain speed and altitude and were apparently safe for the moment. He looked to Fawn, who was once again, adjusting the flame. "So what's the plan?"

She gave an uneasy smile. "Just to put as much distance between us and the *federales* as we can."

"Yeah, but where do you plan on coming down?"

"Well, I can't control where we're going. We're going wherever the wind takes us."

That made sense, but it wasn't what he wanted to hear. "So I guess it's a matter of looking for a soft spot." She nodded.

"Can we stay up until daybreak? It's not going to be easy in this terrain at night."

She shook her head. "We don't have that much fuel."

"So how long before we run out?"

"I don't know, maybe a couple hours." Her words sounded apologetic.

Dan had not enjoyed what he had just heard and showed it in his face. He looked to Fawn and Jack. "You two are the thinkers. What are we gonna do?"

Jack reached over and put his hand on his partner's shoulder. "Don't worry, we've got to come down. The only question is, how hard?"

Dan just shook his head, unable to see humor in the situation. Fawn and Jack exchanged forced smiles.

Jack found himself watching her with fond approval as she tried to judge their height and regulate the burner. There was no question that he loved and respected her. But while he admired her bravery and clever mind, he also felt guilt. She had devised this high-risk plan solely for him, and both she and Dan were putting their lives on the line. He knew that they were beginning to doubt their chances, and he uncharacteristically had no plan. Jack maintained his usual confident demeanor, but actually felt pretty helpless.

Over an hour passed with the sphere climbing higher and reaching stronger and colder wind currents. Fawn did her best to ration the kerosene fuel while continuing to climb. It was the mountains that were the immediate concern. All too soon those towering mountains were getting close, but the balloon was not yet high enough. They were heading straight for the upper slopes. With the speed with which they were approaching, they would hit hard.

Jack turned to Fawn. "Turn that flame up all the way or we're not going to clear this thing!"

Fawn knew he was right, but also knew that they were almost out of fuel. She turned the valve all the way out and the smoky yellow flame rose nearly ten feet up into the sphere. The balloon began to rise a little faster, but not fast enough. The moon had risen a little higher in the sky. It allowed them to see what was coming, and it didn't look good. They were closing fast on the mountain and heading right for the rocky summit. In the last moments, Dan and Fawn moved to the back of the basket, grabbed hold of a rope, and braced for the impact. Then just as Jack put himself in front of Fawn to protect her a little, they felt a sudden, hard pull upwards.

When the wind that had been careening them toward the rocky peak reached the mountain slopes, it was deflected up. That caused an upward current that came none too soon. Jack turned and watched as they rose with the updraft, but were still reeling toward the rocks. He pulled himself closer to Fawn and called out, "Hold on tight, we're going to hit!"

It wasn't a single second before they did. A couple more feet and they would have made it. Instead the basket struck hard against a rocky point that ripped into the basket, causing it to split in two. The burner broke loose from the floor and was instantly tossed out. It was only their tight grip on the ropes that prevented the passengers from going with it. As it was, their bodies were hurled forward with a tremendous jolt, feet first. Then in the next instant, what remained of the basket and its three occupants were driven back and upward, as the balloon rotated forward in reaction from the blow. Yet they continued to climb.

With no source of heat to control their eventual descent, Jack knew he had to get the balloon down in a hurry. If he allowed it to continue to travel up and go beyond the mountain top, they would fall like a stone as the air cooled.

All three of them were still perilously hanging on to the ropes for their lives. Only torn, shredded wicker and the cold night air remained beneath their feet. The balloon continued to heave around from the collision and strong winds. Instinctively, Jack released his right hand from the rope and took the knife from his belt. He placed the blade between his teeth and started climbing, hand over hand, up the rope that encircled the sphere. His weight caused the fabric to bulge inward and push some of the hot air out the bottom, but that was alright with him. His plan was simple and desperate, deflate the balloon before it went higher. When he got about midway up, he took the knife from his mouth. Silk is a particularly tough material, so Jack worked the knife into a stitched seam a foot or so to his right, and started slicing the threads. A few seconds later he had a gaping hole.

Jack sensed that the balloon had stopped climbing. He looked down and saw that they were a hundred feet or so above a fairly flat mesa atop the mountain. There was no way of him seeing how far it was to the end of the mesa and the slopes beyond because the balloon was in his way. It would obviously be better to come down slowly, but he had to get down before they went past the mountain top. He yelled down to Dan and Fawn who were showing the strain of their death grip in their faces. "Can you see the end of this mesa?"

They both peered out into moon-lit night, then Fawn looked up to Jack. "It's too dark, sweetheart. Just get us down." It wasn't so much an answer as it was a plea.

Jack could feel that they were starting to descend, but they were still going forward fast. He slit the seam as he worked his way down using his two feet and left hand on the rope. The balloon began to fall faster and Jack noted the ground coming at them much faster.

Jack slipped the knife back into its sheath and made his way down to what remained of the basket and the two terrified passengers. They were probably only about the height of a two-story house from the ground at that point, a bone-breaking distance, but not fatal. All three looked down at once. They were coming down fast, but not as fast as gravity. Jack then strained his eyes out into the murky darkness ahead. He could just make out the end of the mesa. The mountainside awaited them in seconds at the speed they were going. He called out to Fawn and Dan even though they were right next to him. "We've got to jump. We're about to go off a cliff! Remember how I told you how to tuck into a ball?

You've got to do that when you drop!" Jack turned away from their frightened eyes, looked ahead and then back, giving them one firm nod. "It's time! Go!"

They dropped the ropes, brought their knees to the chest, tucked in their heads, and brought their hands and arms tight around their heads. Jack had only mentioned that position when they asked how he managed to escape the shaft when he rescued the two boys. He had no idea it would someday help them break a fall. They fell onto the grassy mesa nearly at once. Each uttered a painful moan as they struck ground and immediately began to roll. Dan made the most noise, making grunting sounds and cursing until he finally stopped. Fawn did some whimpering as she rolled to a stop. Other than the one involuntary sound he made when he first hit, Jack was silent. He was the first to his feet and rushed over to check on the others.

They had been lucky—the ground had been forgiving. The rains had turned it into a soft clay. Still, Dan had a painful left shoulder, a twisted knee, and a few bruises. Fawn hit her right hip pretty hard and also had some areas of black and blue. Other than being covered with the same wet, brown earth as his partner and sweetheart, Jack was fine. Of course, he was a tough hombre.

After being satisfied that the others were okay, he walked over to the cliff. The balloon was gone, somewhere down deep in the rugged canyon. Another fifty feet from where they landed and they would have been down there too.

It had been close. Too close.

Chapter 21
Going Home

After two blasts from its whistle, the eastbound train slowly rolled out of Tucson Station. Jack and his two weary traveling companions stood on the platform. It was almost noon.

Just over a month had passed since their balloon adventure. The following day had been the worst. A long trek down to the pueblo of Cordoba. They were able to hire horses and a guide there. It was another two weeks of hard riding to reach Acapulco. From there it was a series of merchant ships and ports going north along the mainland coast and into the Sea of Cortez. At Puerto Penasco, they boarded a U.S. cargo vessel. It sailed northwest past Isla Montague and then up the Colorado River as far as Yuma. The Southern Pacific completed the final leg to Tucson.

They had returned without the treasure that lured them to Vera Cruz. Still, Jack felt no regret. He had found the treasure, and that was reward in itself. H

also had about half the money he'd gotten from Madera and LeBoux, and that was more than he had left with. Even the matter of LeBoux turned out better than he had thought. Although he didn't know it at the time, Fawn had asked Madera to report the *Azteca*'s cargo to the authorities. It amused Jack to think of LeBoux and his pirates residing in a Mexican jail.

The livery was a couple blocks up the street and they headed that way. They planned to settle the stable bill, and then head for Mission San Xavier and the Papagos. At nightfall, they would leave for Spirit Feather.

They only got a few paces in that direction when shots rang out. About a block ahead were four cowboys and a young Mexican boy in the middle of the street. The four men were firing their pistols around the boy's feet, making him dance. It was a humiliating and dangerous game, enjoyed only by those holding the guns. It was bad enough when the victim was a man. To inflict it upon a boy, Jack felt, was beneath contempt.

Fawn and Dan were walking to Jack's left. They watched the drama ahead for a moment or two, and then looked to see anger building in Jack's face. When his eyes narrowed and turned cold, there was nothing to do but stay out of the way.

Jack walked right for the boy. The four galoots were around ten steps beyond him, and still firing away. Dan and Fawn drifted over to the side of the street and continued to his left, a little behind. While they followed, Dan explained to her that bloodshed was unlikely. Although Jack's anger was real, his intention was merely to teach them a lesson. Jack, assisted by Dan, was about to play out a game—a game that only worked

because of the reputation of Diamondback McCall. The cowboys were way outclassed. They just didn't know it yet.

Jack came up on the right side of the lad and the shooting stopped. He put his hand on the boy's head, but kept his eyes on the cowboys. Jack spoke softly to him. "It's okay, son. Just wait over there." He pointed toward Fawn and Dan, but the boy hesitated. Jack then added, "*Esperar con mi amigos, por favor.*"

The boy looked that way; Fawn motioned him to her, and he scurried over.

Then there were the usual few moments of silent face-off. The four cowboys held their pistols down at their side as they sized up the tall, dark, and very tough-looking hombre before them.

Jack broke the silence. "Does it really take four of you to scare one little boy?"

The four men stepped closer and fell into a line, nearly shoulder to shoulder. They seemed to have had a few drinks and the comfort of numbers to bolster their confidence. They were all young, none older than thirty. The largest man on the far right answered. "We were just having fun, mister. You have a problem with us having fun?"

"Yeah. Why don't you try it with someone who can shoot back and see how much fun it is?"

"Like you?"

Jack nodded. "Yeah, I'd like to have some fun, too."

The big man snapped his head back a little in surprise. He gave a quick glance at his friends, and then a wry smile curled the corners of his mouth. "You must be crazy, mister. It's four to one and we're already holdin' our guns."

"Well, if you don't like the odds, I can always put one hand behind my back. How's that?"

All four wore a puzzled expression at that point, but the same man answered. "It's your funeral."

Jack moved his left hand around his back as promised, and then gave a single shake of the head. "No, it's yours."

By that time, small crowds were gathering on both sides of the street to watch. Half a dozen were standing behind Dan, Fawn, and the boy.

Then, just as the four seemed to be tensing to make their move, Dan called out from his position between two hitching rails along the storefronts. "Wait a second, boys! The lady and me ain't finished making our bet on this thing."

The big man didn't hide his agitation for the interruption of a private fight. He looked straight at Jack, but answered with a sarcastic tone. "You really think there's a question of the outcome, old-timer."

"Course not. We know who's gonna win. We're bettin' on which way you four fellers are gonna fall." Dan chuckled.

The slightest sign of doubt seem to stir through the cowboys. Once again, the big man did the talking. "What do they call you, mister?"

"You're right. You ought to know who's about to kill you." He stated it matter of factly. "The name's McCall, Jack McCall."

The big man swallowed hard. "You the one they call Diamondback McCall?"

Jack answered with a single nod, and all confidence

in the cowboys evaporated in an instant. They did a bit of squirming and looking to one another before the big fellow spoke up. "There's no need for gunplay. Like I said, we were just havin' fun."

Jack gave the nervous cowboys one last hard stare. "Alright, I guess I don't have to blow your no-good heads off if you're willing to apologize."

They started nodding and, as usual, the big one said it first. "I'm sorry, Mister McCall."

"Not to me!" Jack raised his right hand to cut off further words, and used his left to motion the boy over. Fawn gave him a little nudge in Jack's direction, and he was soon standing beside him.

"This is who you owe an apology." He gestured for the cowboys to come closer. When they got within a few steps of the boy, the word *sorry* started tumbling from their lips.

Jack shook his head. "That doesn't sound sincere to me, boys. On your knees!"

There were a fair amount of chuckles running through the gathered audience by then. The four men didn't like it, but they knelt.

As they did so, Jack added, "Try it in Spanish this time."

One of the men uttered, "*Lo siento.*" They then all followed suit.

Figuring that he had made his point with the four cowboys, Jack stated. "On your feet, boys."

Once standing, they turned to Jack. His words came cold and serious. "If I hear about you boys pulling something like this again, it won't be so easy. *Comprende?*"

They all returned a couple nods.

"Then on your way."

The four men went straight for their horses without a single word. They had been humiliated, and they had it coming. They rode out of town at a gallop as Dan and Fawn strolled out into the street to rejoin Jack.

After reaching into his pants pocket, Jack handed the young boy a silver dollar. His face lit up while stating, "*Gracias, señor.*"

"*Por nada,*" returned Jack, and the lad took off down the street. Fawn was smiling. Dan wore a smirk. She put her arms up around Jack's neck and he lifted her into an embace. She whispered into his ear, "Don't you ever get scared?"

His expression showed some surprise. "There were only four of them," he answered softly while setting her down to her feet.

Dan was looking in the direction of the cowboys' departure, their horses' dust still lingered in the air. He spoke up while turning back to his partner. "I don't think those fellers will be doin' anything wrong for quite a while. But that big galoot was right about one thing. That was fun!"

Jack returned a smile, then added, "Come on, you two. I think we've had enough excitement for a while. Let's go home."